Man of Fortune

ROCHELLE ALERS

NATIONAL BESTSELLING AUTHOR

Man of Fortune

ARABESQUE®

MAN OF FORTUNE

ISBN-13: 978-0-373-83050-3

© 2009 by Rochelle Alers

Printed in U.S.A.

The BEST MEN series

You met Tessa, Faith and Simone—the Whitfields of New York and owners of Signature Bridals—in the WHITFIELD BRIDES series. Now meet three lifelong friends who fulfill their boyhood dream and purchase a Harlem brownstone for their business ventures.

Kyle Chatham, Duncan Gilmore and Ivan Campbell have worked tirelessly to overcome obstacles and achieve professional success, oftentimes at the expense of their personal lives. However, each will meet an extraordinary woman who just might make him reconsider what it means to be the best man.

In *Man of Fate,* high-profile attorney Kyle Chatham's classic sports car is rear-ended by Ava Warrick, a social worker who doesn't think much of lawyers and deeply mistrusts men. Ava expects the handsome attorney to sue her, not come to her rescue after she sustains a head injury in the accident. But Kyle knows he has to prove to Ava that he is nothing like the men in her past—a challenge he is prepared to take on *and* win.

Financial planner Duncan Gilmore's life is as predictable as the numbers on his spreadsheets. After losing his fiancée in the World Trade Center tragedy, he has finally begun dating again. In *Man of Fortune,* Duncan meets Tamara Wolcott—a beautiful and brilliant E.R. doctor with a bad attitude. As their relationship grows, Tamara begins to feel that she is just a replacement for his late fiancée. But Duncan knows that he has to put aside his pride if he's going to convince Tamara to be part of his life.

After the death of his identical twin years ago, psychotherapist Ivan Campbell is a "love 'em and leave 'em" guy who is afraid of commitment. But all of that changes in *Man of Fantasy* when he meets Nayo Goddard at an art gallery, where she is showing her collection of black-and-white photographs. Not only has she gotten Ivan to open up his heart to love again, she is also seeing another man. Ivan knows that he must prove that he is the best man for her, or risk losing her forever.

Yours in romance,

Rochelle Alers

She is more precious than rubies: and all the things
thou canst desire are not to be compared unto her.
—*Proverbs* 3:15

Chapter 1

Duncan Gilmore's head popped up when he heard the two quick taps on the door. A slow smile crinkled around his eyes when he saw a head appear from around the partially opened door.

"Good morning, Kyle. Come on in."

Kyle Chatham opened the door fully and walked into a sun-filled office with a desk, tables, credenza and bookcases made from rosewood and Jamaican mahogany. Everything in the space, from the furnishings to the occupant's attire, conveyed good breeding and elegance. He took a chair beside the desk, which was covered with investment portfolios and a batch of tax returns.

"I heard you were looking for me yesterday. What's up, DG?"

"Are you feeling all right?" Duncan asked.

"Yes. Why?"

"I've never known you to take off on a Monday."

Kyle looped a leg over the opposite knee. "Things have changed now that Jordan Wainwright has joined the firm."

Duncan smiled, exhibiting perfectly aligned white teeth. "I like your new partner, Kyle. At first I thought he wouldn't fit in, but after that TV segment where he called his grandfather a slumlord I have a newfound respect for the poor little rich boy."

Kyle, angling his head, returned his friend's smile. "I felt the same way before Jordan came on board. Representing clients with deep pockets is very different from fighting for the little guy, but Jordan has proven that he is a man for the people. Even though the plaque out front reads Chatham and Wainwright, P.C., Attorneys at Law, and he's accepted a partnership, I'm going to wait until after Labor Day to make it official. It'll give me time to place ads in the local papers and host a reception for a few elected officials and neighborhood residents."

"That sounds good. Jordan's elevation to partner and the added staff should level the playing field when you guys compete with other Harlem law firms."

Kyle ran a hand over his neatly cropped hair. "I don't want to compete, DG. I had enough of that when I worked eighty-hour weeks for Trilling, Carlyle and Browne. Jordan's contribution to the firm has allowed me to pay off half of my share of this building's mortgage and hire additional staff. Taking on a partner has also afforded me a life outside of the office."

"With Ava?"

"Yes, with Ava," Kyle confirmed. "She has a lot of comp time coming, so we've decided to take long weekends together."

"I was looking for you yesterday because one of my clients has season tickets to the Yankee home games. I didn't want to tell him that I'm a Mets fan, so I took them anyway. I know you like the Yankees, and with them playing Boston this weekend it should be quite a series."

"Talk about bad timing. I'm planning to meet Ava's folks."

"Going to meet her parents sounds serious," Duncan said.

Kyle Chatham stared at Duncan. His friend was a magnet for women. Duncan's olive skin, chiseled features and close-cropped curly black hair, his beautifully modulated baritone voice and impeccable attire, made him a standout whenever he entered a room. Kyle was always incredulous that Duncan was totally unaware of the impact he had on women.

"It is. I proposed marriage and she accepted."

Duncan went completely still as he stared at his friend. *I proposed marriage and she accepted.* Those were the exact words he'd said to Kyle and their buddy Ivan one night when he'd asked the two to join him for drinks so that he could share the news that had given him a fitful night's sleep. The difference was that he'd proposed marriage to Kalinda Douglas, but the two never became husband and wife. Fate had interceded on September 11, 2001, when his fiancée died in the terror attacks on the World Trade Center.

Duncan, Kyle Chatham and Ivan Campbell had grown up in the same Harlem public-housing development. His two friends had become as close to him as the brothers he'd never had. The year he turned fourteen, Duncan's single mother had died unexpectedly from a blood clot, and, having never known his father, he went to live with his school-teacher aunt in an upscale Brooklyn neighborhood.

Kyle was the youngest of the trio by several months, having recently celebrated his thirty-ninth birthday. He was tall, and what women referred to as "fine milk chocolate." Duncan detected a change in Kyle over the past few months. Now he knew it had something to do with Ava Warrick.

Rising from his seat, he came around the desk to embrace Kyle, who'd also come to his feet. Duncan pounded his back. "Congratulations. When's the wedding?"

"Not until next year. In fact, Ava wants a winter wedding."

"She wants to get married in New York in the winter?" Duncan asked, a note of incredulity creeping into the question. He sat on the edge of his desk facing Kyle who had sat down again.

A hint of a smile played at the corners of Kyle's mouth. "It wouldn't pose a problem if the wedding were held in Puerto Rico."

"Damn, Kyle! Now you're talking."

Kyle sobered. "I want you to be my best man."

An expression of sadness flitted over Duncan's handsome face before he managed to mask it with a plastic grin. "You're kidding, aren't you?"

He didn't want to relive the time when he'd asked Kyle to become his best man. Kalinda used to e-mail him every morning, counting the days before she became Mrs. Duncan Gilmore. The morning of September 11, the anticipated e-mail never came. Duncan didn't know what was worse—the weeks of waiting or the telephone call from Kalinda's parents that their daughter's body had been recovered in the rubble.

"No, I am not, Duncan."

It wasn't often Kyle called Duncan by his given name because there had been another boy named Duncan who lived in their building, and to differentiate between the two he'd always called Duncan Gilmore DG.

"I thought you would've asked Micah."

Kyle had met Micah Sanborn when he'd become the NYPD officer's law-school mentor. Micah, now a Kings County assistant district attorney, had been promoted to lieutenant when he enrolled in Brooklyn Law School. It'd taken him six years, attending part-time, instead of the normal three to complete his degree. During that time, Kyle had mentored Micah, who had juggled his law-enforcement responsibilities with law school. During his down time Micah would occasionally join Ivan and Duncan at sporting events when Kyle invited him along to unwind.

"Micah's my friend, but you and Ivan are closer to me than my own brother. If you don't want to—"

"Hold up, Kyle," Duncan said, cutting him off. "Did I say I didn't want to be your best man?"

"You didn't say you would," Kyle countered.

He'd asked Duncan to become his best man because he felt closer to him than to Ivan, despite Duncan having moved from Harlem to Brooklyn as a teen. It was Duncan who had always called to see how he was doing, and the routine continued to this day with Duncan stopping by his office several times a week to see how Kyle was doing. Kyle suspected his friend's concern about his well-being had something to do with him losing his mother. Although Duncan said he had noticed signs of distress in his mother, he hadn't called for a doctor or an ambulance until it was too late. He'd come home from school to find Melanie Gilmore on the kitchen floor. The medical examiner had put her time of death at approximately ten that morning.

Now the lifelong friends stared at each other until Duncan inclined his head, breaking the silence. "I'm honored you've asked, and I accept."

Kyle blew out a breath. "Thank you, DG. You don't know what this means to me, because I know it's not going to be easy for you to relive what happened—"

"I'm good, buddy. I'll never forget Kalinda, but each year it gets a little easier. It was the same when I lost my mother." Crossing his arms over his chest, Duncan stared at the pattern on the rug under his shoes. "I have a confession to make." His head came up. "I've had a few sessions with Ivan."

Duncan had been staunchly resistant to seeing a therapist to deal with the grief he felt with the loss of his fiancée. Dr. Ivan Campbell had told Duncan that anytime he wanted to talk—about anything— his door was always open to him. And it had taken Duncan a long time to work up enough nerve to admit that he needed therapy in order to begin dealing with the demons that wouldn't let him get past the tragedies in his life. He wasn't completely free of them yet, but he was getting there.

He'd begun dating again, but none of the relationships had lasted more than a few months. Last weekend he'd asked a woman who was a former college classmate to go out with him. She wasn't his late fiancée, wasn't even remotely close to her. But he did enjoy her company and had told her that, but he hadn't promised he would call her again.

"I'd like to throw a little something at my place to celebrate your engagement. It will be a way for your friends and family and hers to get together and become acquainted with one another."

Leaning forward, Kyle patted Duncan's arm. "I'm going to speak for Ava when I say we'd really appreciate that." In the past, there hadn't been a month when Duncan and Kalinda hadn't hosted a gathering at his Chelsea loft. The soirées were always elegant and well-attended. "What's up with all the financials?" Kyle asked, smoothly changing the topic of conversation.

"You've got to stay on top of the market, especially with clients who are counting on me for their financial security."

Kyle whistled softly. "Damn, maybe I need to have you take another look at my investments."

"Anytime Kyle. Remember, now's the time to make sure your investment strategy is sound." Of his many clients, only Kyle, Ivan Campbell, his aunt Viola Gilmore and a select few got free financial advice.

"On that note," Kyle said, pushing to his feet, "I'll leave you to your spread sheets."

"Congratulations again, buddy."

"Thanks, DG."

Duncan waited until Kyle left before he went back to his computer, estimating it would take the rest of the morning to complete his work. His client, Mrs. Henderson, had neglected to reinvest insurance proceeds after her husband passed away. Unfortunately, she'd ignored the mounting pile of letters from the insurance company until her daughter had discovered them in a drawer with a number of unpaid bills.

Pressing a button on the telephone console, he called his secretary. "Mia, please refer my calls to Auggie."

Augustin Russell, a third-year finance student, worked twenty hours a week when classes were in session and full-time during the summer months. Duncan was seriously considering hiring him after he graduated. Not only was he bright, but he was also very ambitious, reminding Duncan of himself when he'd begun his MBA studies. Not only had Duncan earned an MBA, but earlier that spring he'd applied and been accepted into a joint JD/MBA degree program.

His graduate-studies concentration was venture capital financing and asset management. It was as if he had a sixth sense when it came to buying and selling stocks and bonds. He knew intuitively when to sell stocks before they declined, and he knew the MBA coursework with a focus on investment strategies had been crucial to his success in monitoring his own and his clients' investment portfolios.

Like Kyle, Duncan had tired of working sixteen-hour days to make money for an investment company. Following the advice he'd given his clients, he invested heavily in the tech market, then sold his shares before they bottomed out. The return on his investments was staggering and gave him the impetus to set up his own financial-planning company.

He purchased loft space, renovated it and moved from the apartment in his aunt's downtown Brooklyn brownstone to a four-bedroom, three-and-a-half-bath condo giving him more than three thousand square feet for living and entertaining.

Now, working on Mrs. Henderson's problem, Duncan lost track of time and everything going on around him but the figures on the computer program.

He was interrupted once when his secretary brought him a cup of coffee. His smile of gratitude conveyed his appreciation. It was minutes before three in the afternoon when the final spread sheet came out of the printer that sat on a corner of the L-shaped, glass-topped desk.

Gathering up the pages, he put them in his monogrammed leather briefcase that had been a graduation gift from his aunt. A schoolteacher by profession, Viola Gilmore valued education as much as she valued life itself. She had repeatedly emphasized the importance of a good education until Duncan was convinced he'd been brain-washed.

Viola had cried when he'd told her he was moving out of the brownstone, but she'd eventually come around. It took Duncan several months of living completely on his own to realize he'd become the son Viola had never had. What he didn't and couldn't explain to his aunt was that, despite having his own apartment in the brownstone, he'd felt un-comfortable bringing his dates home with him. Never one to boast about his sexual conquests, he'd always kept his personal life very, very private. Ivan and Kyle were shocked when he disclosed he'd proposed marriage to Kalinda, because up until that time neither had met her or heard him mention her.

Duncan shut down the computer, straightened up his desk, slipped into his suit jacket, picked up his briefcase and walked out of his office. Mia Humphrey swiveled around in her chair when he strode past her.

"Good afternoon, Duncan."

He smiled without turning around. "Go home, Mia."

A rush of blood suffused her olive complexion. "I'm going."

The year before, Duncan had instituted summer work hours to allow his secretary and accounting clerk more time to enjoy the warmer weather. Office hours during July and August were nine to three Monday through Thursday and nine to one on Friday.

Duncan knew that Mia, a young single mother, had taken a more than friendly interest in his assistant. Even though he didn't approve of office romances, he had no intention of interfering in the personal lives of his employees. After all, both were consenting adults.

He walked through the renovated brownstone's reception area, where a man and several women lounged in chairs watching the wall-mounted flat-screen television, and out into the blistering heat. Spending hours in the building's air-conditioned interior hadn't prepared him for the hazy, hot and humid summer weather.

Aside from working for himself, Duncan's pride came as one-third owner of the renovated brown-stone in Harlem's Mount Morris Park Historic District. His office occupied the first floor, Kyle's law firm the second and Ivan's counseling center was set up on the third floor. The street level had been reconfigured to include a gym with a locker room and showers, a modern state-of-the-art kitchen and a dining room. The year before, a game room with pool and Ping-Pong tables had been added, along with several pinball machines and a large-screen television for video games.

Strolling down the tree-lined block, Duncan stopped at the corner and flagged down a taxi. He was loath to ride the subway, not wanting to endure the suffocating heat and the less-than-affable attitudes of straphangers packed into subway cars like sardines.

Sliding into the rear seat of the air-conditioned cab, he gave the driver his destination. "Nineteenth and Park Avenue South." The cabbie took off, heading downtown while Duncan closed his eyes. The ride was long enough for him to take a power nap.

"I'm going to have to put you out here, mister."

Duncan opened his eyes, peering out the side window. It seemed as if he'd just closed his eyes. The taxi driver had pulled over on Park Avenue South, but it was blocks from his destination. "I asked for Nineteenth Street."

The cabbie turned to stare at the man in a suit and tie knotted to his throat despite the ninety-degree temperatures. "I can't go any farther. The streets are closed. There was a water-main break yesterday."

Duncan paid the fare, giving the cabbie a generous tip, and walked the remaining two blocks to an opulent Gramercy Park apartment building, where he gave the doorman his name, adding, "Mrs. Henderson is expecting me."

The doorman rang Genevieve Henderson's apartment, speaking softly into the telephone receiver. He nodded to Duncan. "You can go up. Mrs. Henderson is in apartment 12D. The elevator for even-numbered floors is on your left."

Duncan nodded, smiling. "Thank you."

The doorman inclined his head. "You're welcome, sir."

"Are you certain you don't want another glass of
tea?"

Duncan smiled at the quirky woman who at one
time had been wardrobe mistress for the American
Ballet Company. "I'm quite certain, Mrs. Henderson." He held up his glass. "Two is usually my limit."

She wagged a bejeweled finger at him. She wore
a ring on each one of her fingers, including her
thumbs. The precious and semi-precious stones
were sizeable, the designs reminiscent of estate
jewelry. "I thought I told you to call me Genevieve,"
she scolded. "Pshaw, I can see it if you'd had two
double martinis, but not iced tea."

Duncan curbed the urge to roll his eyes. "I try to
limit my caffeine intake."

"You're in luck today. I used decaffeinated tea."

He took a surreptitious glance at his watch. It was
after five, he wanted to go home, take a shower and
relax, but Mrs. Henderson—no, Genevieve—had
held him hostage with her stories about the famous
dancers who'd performed with the ballet company
where she'd worked for more than thirty years.

Sitting up straighter, he reached for his suit
jacket. "I really must go, Genevieve."

"Do you have a date?"

The question caught Duncan off-guard as he stared at the woman with the cotton-candy-pink curls. Rising to his feet, he slipped into his jacket and reached for the case filled with the papers for her to sign. "No, I don't. And as much I've enjoyed talking with you, I must leave."

Genevieve's dark eyebrows lifted slightly. "You sound so formal. You were that way when you took my Lucy to your senior prom. I guess that comes from living with Viola. She is the primmest and most proper woman I've ever met. She made everyone on the block address her as Miss Gilmore rather than Viola."

Duncan smiled. "That's my aunt." He made his way across the living room to the door, Genevieve following. "Please call me if you get any more letters from the insurance company."

"I can't be bothered with that nonsense. I'll give them to Lucy to give to you."

He wanted to tell Genevieve that her rental properties afforded her a very comfortable lifestyle. She'd sold her Brooklyn brownstone and moved into Manhattan after her husband of forty-two years had passed away. What Duncan couldn't understand was how a woman could live with a man for more than four decades, yet not know he owned several parcels of rental property in Florida. Her late husband's business partner deposited the rent checks, mailed her a check each quarter, less real estate taxes, but had neglected to send Genevieve the bank statements. When Lucy questioned the man, his response had been that he forgot. He forgot—and as a result Duncan had taken on another client.

He and thrice-married Lucretia Henderson had attended the same high school. Duncan had taken her to the senior prom when her date came down with chicken pox, and they'd been reunited the year before at their twentieth high-school reunion. A long sigh escaped his lips when the door closed behind him.

Do you have a date? No, he didn't have a date, but he wanted to go home and unwind after what had become a month of nonstop work. Perhaps he would even think about taking a day off to do absolutely nothing.

Duncan hadn't taken a real vacation in more than three years. The last time was when he'd accompanied his aunt on a cross-country train ride to the Pacific Northwest before they boarded a cruise ship for Alaska.

He pushed the elevator button and made a mental note to stop by a travel agency and pick up some brochures. Within seconds, the doors opened and he met the startled gaze of a woman buttoning her blouse.

"You missed a few," he said softly as he walked into the car.

Tamara Wolcott glanced down at her chest. Not only had she missed several buttons, but she hadn't put them in the corresponding buttonholes. There was no doubt the stranger could see her bra and everything inside it.

She rolled her eyes at him. "Thanks!"

Duncan couldn't stop the smile stealing its way across his face. "You're welcome. That's what happens when you have to dress in a hurry," he drawled facetiously.

Turning her back, Tamara unbuttoned then buttoned her blouse again. "It's not what you think," she snapped.

"How do you know what I'm thinking?" Duncan asked.

"It was your snarky comment about getting dressed in a hurry."

His smile faded. "Is there such a word as *snarky?*"

"Yes, there is," she retorted. "Look it up—" Whatever Tamara was going to say died on her lips when the elevator came to an abrupt halt midway between the first and second floors. The emergency light came on and she slapped the emergency button, while muttering a colorful expletive.

Duncan moved over to the panel and released the emergency button, hoping the action would restart the elevator. He waited a full thirty seconds, and then pushed it again. The piercing sound was annoying *and* deafening. He released it. "It looks like we're stuck."

"You don't say, Einstein."

"Ditch the attitude, lady," he countered nastily. "It's not going to solve anything. It's apparent someone in the lobby heard the bell, so it shouldn't be long before we're out of here."

Tamara opened her mouth to deliver a sarcastic comeback to the man who not only looked good but also smelled incredibly delicious. He was tall, slender and impeccably dressed in a lightweight gray suit, white shirt and silk tie in varying shades of gray, black and white. His cropped, raven-black curly hair, smooth olive skin and intense light-brown eyes under arching black eyebrows were mesmerizing. A straight nose and firm mouth added to what was an arresting face. And she was annoyed with herself because she found him so physically attractive.

"I hope it's not going to take too long because I have to go to work."

Leaning against a wall, Duncan crossed his arms over his chest. "Where is work?"

Tamara closed her eyes for several seconds. "I work in a hospital." She glared at the man who didn't appear in the least perturbed that they were stuck in an elevator in a Manhattan highrise. "Can you please push the emergency button again?" She couldn't control the slight quiver in her voice.

Duncan didn't move as he continued to stare at the woman with the voluptuous body and sexy voice. If he had ever fantasized about getting trapped in an elevator with someone, then this was his dream come true. She was tall, at least five-nine or ten with flawless tawny skin, and she had pulled her hair into a ponytail ending midway down her back. Her mouth matched her body. It was full, lush and temptingly curved. If the eyes were a mirror into someone's soul, then hers radiated anger and resentment. The large, dark, slanting orbs gave off sparks that didn't bode well for anyone on the receiving end of her rage. He forced himself not to look at the swell of breasts under a man's white shirt. A pair of stretch jeans and black leather mules completed her dressed-down look.

He forced a smile. "I'm certain someone heard the bell."

Tamara took a quick breath. "How do you know that for certain, Mister-Know-It-All?"

Duncan's smile faded. She was back with the bad attitude. His temper flared. "Push the damn button yourself if you think that's going to move the elevator."

Tamara reached for the button at the same time voices came somewhere outside the door. "We're stuck in here," she shouted.

"Hold on, miss. We're going to try and get you out," said a muffled voice. "Someone in the Con Ed work crew cut a feeder cable and…" His voice trailed off.

"A feeder cable," she repeated. "That means there's no electricity."

Duncan gestured to the overhead emergency light. "At least we're not in the dark."

Tamara reached into an oversized leather tote and took out her cell phone. "I hope I can get a signal in here." She exhaled a breath. "Thank goodness." Scrolling through her directory she pushed speed dial. "This is Dr. Wolcott," she said identifying herself when a clerk answered the phone. "I'm scheduled to cover the six o'clock shift for Dr. Shelton, but right now I'm stuck in an elevator in a building on Park Avenue South. Tell Dr. Killeen I'll be in once someone gets me out of here."

"I'll let—wait a minute, Dr. Wolcott, there's a special news bulletin coming across the television. The power is out in most of Gramercy Park. Is that where you are?"

"Yes."

"I'll let Dr. Killeen know that you'll be late."

"Make certain you do."

Tamara ended the call and looked at the man staring back at her with an amused expression. She didn't know what was so funny. They were trapped in a space less than six feet wide that was getting hotter with each passing moment.

"What's so funny?"

Duncan straightened. "Are you usually so brusque, Dr. Wolcott?"

She looked down at the toes of his polished shoes. "No, I'm not. Right now I'm a little stressed out. I'm sorry if I was rude to you, Mr...."

"Duncan."

Her head came up. "Does Duncan have a last name?"

"It's Gilmore." He extended his hand. "Does Dr. Wolcott have a first name?"

She shook his hand, noting the palm was smooth to the touch. "It's Tamara."

"Tamara," he repeated. "What does it mean?"

"It's Hebrew for palm tree."

"It's very pretty."

Tamara smiled for the first time. "Thank you." She offered him her cell phone. "I was told that half the neighborhood is without electricity. You can use my phone if you need to make a call."

"Thanks, but no thanks."

Her eyebrows lifted slightly. "Isn't there someone you would want to know where you are?"

"No."

Tamara's eyes narrowed. "Do you live in this building?"

"No," Duncan repeated. "I was just leaving a client. Do you live here?"

"I wish. I live in an incredibly overpriced East Village walkup."

"Living in Manhattan is practically prohibitive."

"You can say that again," she drawled. "Where do you live, Duncan?"

"Chelsea." He smiled when Tamara whistled. "It's not quite Park Avenue or Sutton Place, but it's getting there."

"Where in Chelsea do you live?"

"Twenty-First between Tenth and Eleventh."

"Isn't that near Chelsea Piers?" she asked.

Duncan nodded. "I can see it from my bedroom window. Have you ever been there?"

"Unfortunately, I haven't," Tamara said truthfully.

She'd worked double shifts for the past four years to pay off her student loans *and* recoup the monies she'd saved before her ex-husband had emptied their joint bank account with the intent of doubling the money at the blackjack table.

"My hectic schedule doesn't allow for much socializing."

Duncan glanced at his watch. They'd been in the elevator for ten minutes. He shrugged out of his suit jacket, let it fall to the floor of the elevator car, and then sat down on it. If he was going to spend any more time confined to such a small space then he planned to relax.

Tamara stared at him as if he'd taken leave of his senses. "What do you think you're doing?"

A pair of clear amber-colored eyes met a pair of coal-black ones. "What does it look like? I'm taking a load off my feet." He offered his hand. "Come sit down. It's not as hot down here."

"That's because hot air rises," Tamara countered.

Again, he ignored her quip. "Sit down, Tamara."

Resting her hands on her hips, she glared down at him. "Are you familiar with the word *please?*"

Duncan didn't drop his hand. Baring his teeth, he flashed a facetious smile. "Please, Dr. Wolcott, won't you sit down?"

She rolled her eyes. "I'm only Dr. Wolcott at the hospital. Otherwise it's Tamara."

Half rising, Duncan eased Tamara down to sit beside him on his jacket. He caught the scent of her perfume. They sat silently as the seconds ticked off to minutes. He checked his watch again. Another quarter of an hour had passed. If Genevieve Henderson hadn't insisted he stay he would've been home by now. It took about half an hour to walk from Gramercy Park to where he lived in Chelsea.

A slight smile tilted the corners of his mouth when Tamara rested her head on his shoulder. "How are you holding up?" he asked after a prolonged silence.

"I'm okay."

Tamara wanted to tell Duncan that she was more than okay. His tailored shirt concealed a lean, hard body. *Soft hands, hard body,* she mused, wondering what he did for a living. It was the first time in a very long time that she'd felt so comfortable with a man. After a rocky marriage and less-than-amicable divorce she'd sworn off men. She had dated but hadn't slept with a man since her divorce, and at thirty-two she was more than content not to change her lifestyle or marital status.

Duncan shifted into a more comfortable position. "Why did you decide to become a doctor?"

"It's a long story, Duncan."

"We have nothing but time and you have a captive audience. Pardon the pun."

Tamara laughed. The sultry sound filled the confined space, sending shivers up Duncan's spine. He suspected the woman pressed to his side was unaware of how sexy her voice, laugh and curvy body were concealed under a man's shirt and body-hugging jeans.

"I became a doctor to spite my mother."

Chapter 2

Tamara couldn't believe she'd just told Duncan something she'd never told another living soul—and that included the man whom she'd believed was the love of her life before he'd become the bane of her existence. It didn't matter what she said to Duncan Gilmore because after they were rescued from the elevator the odds were she would never see him again.

"Spite her how?" Duncan asked.

How, she mused, had she not noticed the low, sensual timbre of the voice of the man pressed against her side? Physically he was perfect, and she felt an unexpected jolt of envy for the woman who claimed him for herself.

"I spent all of my childhood and the beginning of my adult life trying to get the approval of my overly critical mother. I'm the youngest of three girls and my sisters Renata and Tiffany are black Barbie dolls, and there wasn't a day when my mother didn't remind me that not only was I taller but I also weighed much more than they did."

"How much *do* they weigh?"

"Tiffany claims she's one-ten, while Renata admits to being one-thirteen."

"How tall are they?"

"Both are five-eight."

"Aren't they anorexic?"

Tamara forced a smile. "I'd say they are. At thirty-six and thirty-eight they wear a size zero and a size two after having several children. But Mother says they're perfect. They had debutante cotillions, but I was denied one because my mother claimed she didn't want me looking like I was wearing a white tent."

Duncan stared at Tamara's hands, which were balled up in fists. He didn't know whether she'd been an overweight teen, but she definitely wasn't now. Her figure was full, rounded and undeniably womanly. Everything about Tamara Wolcott was feminine and as close to perfection as a woman could get.

"Were you overweight?"

"No. I was five-ten and weighed one forty-five.

My pediatrician constantly told Mother I wasn't overweight. But she has her own set of standards that were and are totally unrealistic. The Wolcotts have been educators for more than a century, so when I graduated from college it was expected that I go into teaching. I never told anyone that I wanted to be a doctor, so I took a lot of math and science courses pretending that I planned to teach science or math.

"My oldest sister was getting married and Mother was so focused on making certain Renata would have the wedding of the season that she didn't have time to monitor my life. I took the GMAT and the MCAT, and got nearly perfect scores. Meanwhile I'd applied to medical schools."

"Where did you go?"

"New York University. I'd been accepted at SUNY Stony Brook, but decided against it because that's where my father is head of the sociology department."

"Did you live on campus?"

Tilting her chin, Tamara stared at Duncan. "Not the first year. Getting up before dawn and commuting from Long Island into Manhattan five days a week left me with little or no time for studying. Once I was approved for campus housing my life changed and I swore never to live at home again."

Resting his hand over her clasped ones, Duncan gave it a gentle squeeze. "Were you screaming, 'Free at last?'"

"How did you know?"

"I knew a few people who had parents who refused to cut the umbilical cord."

Tamara laid her head against his shoulder again as if it was something she'd done countless times. "Did it happen with you, Duncan?"

"No. I think it's different with guys, because we're expected to grow up and be men, while daddies think of their daughters as little girls even when they're grown women."

He recalled the in-depth conversation he'd had with Kalinda's father who'd said he expected his daughter to be still a virgin when she married. What the older man hadn't known was that Duncan wasn't the first man who'd slept with her, but there was no way he was going to reveal that to his future father-in-law.

"Unfortunately the double standard is still alive and kicking," Tamara drawled, adding an unladylike snort. "I hope you don't make distinctions between your children whether they're girls or boys."

"If I had children, I doubt that I would consciously treat them differently. What I can say for certain is that if some guy decides he's going to take advantage of my daughter, he'd better make funeral arrangements, because I'd definitely take him out."

"But you *are* making a distinction, Duncan," she argued softly.

"Do you have any children, Tamara?"

"No."

"Since we're both childless, then the topic is moot."

"Because you say so," she retorted.

Duncan groaned. "Tamara, Tamara, Tamara. Why are you so argumentative?"

Tamara pulled her hands away. "You think I am?"

"Yes."

She sobered. "Sorry. I didn't realize I came off sounding that way."

It was Duncan's turn to be repentant. "Perhaps I used the wrong word. I should've said you appear defensive."

"Don't tell me you're a therapist."

"Nope."

The seconds ticked off. "What are you?" Tamara asked when he seemed reluctant to answer her question.

"I'm a financial planner."

"Are you a financial planner or an accountant?"

"I'm both."

"Do you practice accounting?"

Duncan shook his head. "Not in the traditional sense."

"Why did you get an accounting degree if not to practice or teach?"

"It's a long story."

Tamara gave him a winning smile. "Didn't you say we have nothing but time? And besides, you have a captive audience."

Duncan returned her smile with a dazzling one of his own, unaware of the effect it had on the woman beside him. "I'll tell you on one condition."

She gave him a skeptical look. "What's that?"

"If you snap at me again, then you'll have to take me out to dinner. Then I'll tell you what you want to know."

"And if I don't?"

"Then I'll take you out."

"What are you going to say to your wife or girl-friend about taking a strange woman to dinner?"

Duncan angled his head as he met Tamara's eyes. There was amusement shimmering in the black orbs. "I don't have a wife or girlfriend, so the issue is also moot."

Tamara gave him a long, penetrating stare. "I should've met you years ago before I was going through what became a very contentious divorce."

"Are you married now?"

"No. And I've never been happier."

"You didn't like being married?"

"I loved being married," she admitted. "It was just how it ended. My ex cleaned out our joint bank accounts, and because I wanted to be rid of the bastard I gave him our Upper Eastside co-op. And if that wasn't enough he also wanted my dog."

"Did you give up the pooch?"

Tamara's eyes filled with tears when she remembered the fluffy white bichon frise that had been her constant companion. Edward Bennett had refused to sign off on the divorce papers until she gave up the apartment and the dog, then he promptly sold the co-op and gave *her* pet to an ex-wife she knew nothing about.

"Yes. It was either give up Snowflake or go to prison for murder." Her delicate jaw hardened. "I lost many sleepless nights thinking of the different ways I could take him out."

Duncan winced. "It was that bad?"

"I was at the lowest point in my life and he knew it. I'd just completed my PGY-3. Third-year residency," Tamara explained when Duncan gave her a confused stare. "I was just recovering from taking the fourth part of the medical boards and my nerves were shot from working thirty-six hours with little or no sleep. I suspected something was wrong because Edward started complaining that we never got to see one another, and when we did, I paid more attention to Snowflake than I did to him."

"Didn't he know that when he married a doctor?"

"He knew exactly what it took for me to become a doctor. He'd been through the same course of study. But it was apparent he'd forgotten."

Duncan went completely still. "He's also a doctor?"

Tamara nodded. "We met during my first year in medical school. He was my anatomy professor," she said after a comfortable silence. "I was twenty, impressionable and very, very gullible. Edward was fifty-six, elegant, erudite, and I didn't know at the time that I was to become his third wife, or that his daughter was also a medical student at Harvard."

"How did your parents react to your marrying a man more than twice your age?"

"My father was upset because he and Edward were about the same age, but Mother, being the social climber that she is, was thrilled that her daughter had chosen to marry a doctor."

"How long were you married?"

"Six years, and in the end I walked away with what I'd brought into the marriage—the clothes on my back. The apartment was his and he'd given me Snowflake as a gift."

"What about alimony, Tamara? You were at least entitled to that."

"I thought I was until my lawyer told me that Edward was paying alimony to two ex-wives and college tuition for three children."

Duncan was momentarily speechless in his surprise. It was no wonder she was angry, abrasive. Tamara had married a stranger, a man who'd managed to conceal his past until it had caught up with him. Was her ex that wily, or was Tamara that naive? It was probably the latter. If she was engrossed in med school, studying for the boards and working around the clock as a resident, then delving into her husband's past was not a priority for her.

"Do you still see your ex?" he asked.

"Thankfully no. He transferred to a small medical school in Rhode Island."

"Has he remarried?" Duncan teased.

"I hope not," Tamara countered. "Being married to Edward taught me one thing—never to put all of my eggs in one basket. When he emptied the bank accounts he took the money my grandparents had given me as a gift for my education. I had to take out a loan to get an apartment because I knew I couldn't continue to live with Edward, and also to have enough to pay a lawyer to handle the divorce. After I got my license, I worked double and triple shifts to pay off the loans."

"Your lawyer should've forced him to return your money."

Tamara heard the censure in Duncan's normally melodic tone. He probably believed she'd given up too easily, that she'd permitted a man to take advantage of her. "There was no money for him to return, Duncan. He'd lost every penny in Atlantic City."

"If he was that broke, then your attorney should've insisted he sell the co-op and return your money."

"Easy, Duncan," she teased, "you're snapping at me again."

His face was a mask of icy anger. "You were screwed twice. Once by your ex and again by your lawyer."

"Don't worry. It's never going to happen again."

"Because you say so, Tamara?"

"Yes, because I'll never trust another man as long as I live."

"Do you think that's fair?" Duncan asked.

"What?"

"That you lump all men into the same category."

"It's not about what's fair and not fair," Tamara countered. "It's about how men have treated me."

"It's how you have let men treat you," Duncan said in a quiet voice.

"Oh, so you're blaming me for not knowing that my ex hid the fact that he'd been married before? Or that he'd had children from his previous marriages? It didn't dawn on me to do a background check on him."

Tamara inhaled and held her breath before letting it out slowly. The heat inside the elevator car was stifling and she was beginning to perspire—something she detested. She'd gone to a colleague's apartment in the highrise to shower and change her clothes instead of going to her aprtment in the East Village. If she'd known she was going to be stuck in an elevator, then taking the downtown subway several stops would've been preferable, even though she avoided riding the subway whenever possible. Her usual mode of transportation was either a bus or a taxi, the latter only in an emergency.

Despite the build-up of heat in the elevator, Duncan draped an arm over Tamara's shoulders, pulling her closer. "I'm not beating up on you, Tamara. I just want you to realize that all men aren't like your ex or the lawyer who swindled you out of your money while not bothering to represent you."

Tilting her chin, Tamara stared into the large, clear brown eyes with the dark centers. "If I'd known you, would you have advocated for me?"

"If I'd been your financial planner, I would've told you to keep your money separate from your husband's, especially if it was money that you'd accumulated before the marriage."

She closed her eyes for several seconds. "It was only after I'd completed my undergraduate studies when I told my parents that I'd applied to and been accepted into medical school that they changed their minds about me becoming a doctor. Mother and Daddy put up the money for my first two years of medical school and both sets of grandparents covered the last two. My only consolation was that I wasn't saddled with having to pay back six-figure student loans."

"You were luckier than most students. I have clients who make more than adequate salaries but they're still paying off student loans."

"Who do you work for?"

"I work for myself," Duncan said smoothly, with no expression on his face.

Tamara was slightly taken aback. She didn't know why, but she'd expected him to mention one of the major investment companies. "Do you work from a home office?"

He pointed to her left side. "Scoot over a little and reach into the breast pocket of my jacket. There's a case with my business cards. Take one."

Seeing the label stitched on the inside of Duncan's suit jacket and the monogrammed silver card case told Tamara all she needed to know about the man sitting beside her. Duncan Gilmore treated himself very well. She took out a card, smiling. It was made of vellum with raised black lettering.

"DGG Financial Services, LLP," she read aloud. "Is your office uptown?"

Duncan smiled. "It's smack dab in good old Harlem, U.S.A."

Tamara heard the pride in his voice. "I take it you're a Harlem native?"

"Born and raised. At least until I was fourteen. Then I moved to Brooklyn."

"If you work in Harlem, then why don't you live there?" she asked.

"That's another story for another time."

A slight frown creased Tamara's smooth forehead. "What are you talking about?"

"I snapped at you, Tamara, therefore I owe you dinner."

She waved a hand. "You don't have—"

"But I'd like to," he interrupted.

A warning shiver snaked its way up Tamara's

spine. She shuddered visibly despite the heat. There was something in the way Duncan Gilmore was looking at her that made her feel uncomfortable. "I can't, Duncan." she whispered.

"Why can't you, Tamara?"

"I have to work."

"Do you work twenty-four/seven?"

"No but—"

Duncan held up a hand, cutting her off. "All I'm asking for is one dinner date."

She gave him a sidelong glance, finding it hard to understand why a man who looked like Duncan Gilmore would insist she go out with him. She didn't know what his motive was, but he'd find out soon enough that Tamara Wolcott was nothing like the wide-eyed young woman who'd succumbed to her med school teacher's influence. Duncan claimed he didn't have a wife or girlfriend, but he hadn't said he was into women. Perhaps he was gay, and if that were true then she was in luck. The last thing she needed was a physical relationship with a man, because each time she slept with one it ended badly.

Some women could have an affair and when it ended they were able to move on. But Tamara always found herself getting too emotionally attached and wanting more. And the more was total commitment. In that way she and Edward were alike. He had confessed that he didn't like sleeping around, and when he did sleep with a woman he usually wanted to marry her. However, what Tamara hadn't known was that she was the third Mrs. Edward Bennett and probably wouldn't be the last.

She forced a smile. "All right, Duncan. I'll go out with you."

A frown distorted his beautiful male face. "Why do you make it sound as if you're doing me a favor?"

"Aren't I?" Tamara drawled.

The seconds ticked off as they stared at each other. A smile replaced Duncan's scowl. "Yes, you are. And I thank you for accepting."

"You're most welcome." She glanced at the card again. "Which number should I use to call you?"

Duncan held out his hand. "Please give me the card." Reaching into the pocket of his shirt, he took out a pen and wrote down a number on the back of the card, then returned it to Tamara. "That's my home number. If I don't pick up, then leave a number where I can call you back."

"I…" Her words trailed off with the sudden movement of the elevator. The overhead lights came on as the car descended slowly. Tamara and Duncan shared a smile. "Free at last," she whispered.

Duncan wasn't ready to lose Tamara's company. She looked nothing like the women he was normally attracted to, but something about her was intrinsically feminine despite her overtly tough, in-your-face attitude. She'd been deceived, hurt, was in pain, and it was apparent she had no desire to let go of that pain.

It was also apparent she had no use for men, either, believing all they were out for was to take advantage of her. But Duncan wanted to prove her wrong. There were good men, those who loved their wives and their children, men who'd chosen not to marry, yet who remained faithful and supportive boyfriends.

All she had to do was meet his boyhood friends Ivan Campbell and Kyle Chatham. The three of them had taken an oath when they were young to remain connected always, to stay away from the drugs that plagued Harlem and to one day own one of the stately brownstones along the many tree-lined streets in the historic neighborhood. And to their amazement, their dreams had come true.

Pushing to his feet, he extended his hand and pulled Tamara up with minimal effort. "How long will it take you to get to the hospital?"

She checked her watch. It was six-ten. "Probably about twenty minutes."

He slipped into his jacket, then leaned over to pick up his case. "May I interest you in sharing a cab?"

"No thank you. I'll walk."

Duncan wanted to tell her that she was already late for her shift, but held his tongue. He'd gotten her to agree to have dinner with him, and given her track record with men, he considered himself quite fortunate.

The snail-like movement of the elevator came to a complete stop at the first floor and the doors opened. Several workmen in coveralls were milling in the area, along with the doorman.

"Are you all right, Dr. Wolcott?" the doorman asked, as lines of concern creased his forehead.

Tamara hoisted her tote over her shoulder. "Yes. Thank you for asking."

Duncan, resting his hand at the small of her back, escorted her across the lobby and out onto the street. Barricades blocked off the street, barring vehicular traffic as emergency personnel from the FDNY, NYPD and Con Ed filled the street and sidewalk.

He walked with Tamara to Twenty-Third Street. Smiling, he stared at her natural beauty in the light of the sun that was sinking lower in the summer sky, casting shadows over the towering buildings that made up the Manhattan skyline.

"This is where I leave you."

Tamara looked at Duncan—really looked at him for the first time in broad daylight and felt as if something had sucked the air from her lungs. His chiseled face was breathtaking and his eyes mesmerizing. If he was gay, then she felt a profound sadness that he wouldn't pass on his incredible genes. And although he'd spent more than half an hour in a stuffy elevator he looked as if he were ready to start the day, not end it. He hadn't bothered to loosen his tie, or undo the French cuffs of his shirt. The only concession he'd made was to take off his custom-tailored jacket to place it on the floor of the elevator, reminding her of a modern-day Sir Walter Raleigh removing his cloak so the queen wouldn't have to navigate a puddle.

"Thank you for the company, even if it was unsolicited." A slight lifting of his silky eyebrows was the only reaction to her slight reproach. "And I will call you," she added, hoping to counter her flippant comment.

Duncan's impassive expression masked his annoyance. She just wouldn't let up, and at that moment he chided himself for asking Tamara to go out with him. "Good night, Tamara." Turning on his heel, he headed west, leaving her staring at his back.

"Good night, Duncan." She groaned inwardly. Even his walk was unique. There was just a light dip in his stroll to make it sexy. Gay or straight, Duncan Gilmore was fine as hell!

What's wrong with you girl!

Tamara silently chided herself for her insensitivity. Duncan had been nothing but cordial to her and she'd attacked him as if he'd insulted her. When, she thought, would she ever rid herself of the lingering anger of her failed marriage? She'd been divorced for four years, and now, at the age of thirty-two, she should be more than ready to turn the page and get on with her life.

She walked uptown to Thirty-Fourth and headed east to First Avenue. Tamara found working in the emergency trauma unit of the city's oldest municipal hospital frenetic yet rewarding. On any given day or night there was a consistent influx of patients. Some were treated and released, while others were taken to a tertiary unit for a higher level of care.

The Bellevue Hospital Center's efficient state-of-the-art E.R. and level-one trauma center were designed to deliver complete twenty-four-hour, seven-day-a-week medical care. With close to one hundred thousand emergency-room visits a year, Tamara and her colleagues were prepared for psychiatric emergencies as well as neurological, toxicological, cardiac and neonatal emergencies.

She loved everything about medicine from studying to healing. During her interview before being admitted to med school, she'd been asked why she wanted to become a doctor. Her answer was that she had a passion for learning, an intellectual curiosity about medicine and a strong willingness to help others. It must have been the right response because the interview process ended minutes after it'd begun. She knew her MCAT score and undergraduate grades were high enough to get her into most leading medical schools, but Tamara realized it was her unabashed passion for healing that showed through during the interview.

When she received her acceptance letter it swept

away all of the insecurities she'd had growing up. It no longer mattered that she wasn't as cute and petite as her sisters, or that her mother had referred to her as "my ugly duckling." None of that mattered because she was going to become a doctor.

Reaching into her tote bag, she turned off her cell phone and took out her stethoscope and ID badge, clipping it to the pocket of the shirt she'd borrowed from another doctor. She'd been too exhausted to ride the bus to her apartment. She'd stopped at a CVS to pick up toothpaste, a toothbrush and deodorant, and then went to a clothing store to buy undergarments and a pair of jeans.

She'd managed to get four hours of sleep before she had to get up and start again. Sleep had become a precious commodity for Tamara, as important as breathing. Whenever she put her head on a pillow her intention was to get at least four hours of uninterrupted sleep. And she'd become quite adept at taking power naps. Ten to twenty minutes was all she needed to reenergize herself.

She walked into the E.R. and down a corridor where hospital personnel stored their personal effects. Tamara placed her tote bag in a locker with a combination lock. She went to a storage closet, selected a pair of scrubs and a white lab coat and then clocked in. Ten minutes later she stood over a gunshot victim handcuffed to the gurney while two uniformed police officers waited for her to remove the bullet lodged in the fleshy part of his thigh. Luckily for her patient, the bullet had missed the femoral artery or he would've bled out and died.

She lost track of time as she treated a patient in cardiac arrest, one with a knife wound, a woman who'd jumped from a third-story window to escape an abusive boyfriend, a college student with a suspected case of meningitis and an adolescent boy bitten by a venomous snake he'd hidden in a fish tank in his bedroom closet.

She worked nonstop until midnight, then went into the doctor's lounge to take a break. She flopped down on a saggy sofa and closed her eyes with the intention of taking a quick nap.

"Tamara, are you asleep?"

She opened her eyes to find Rodney Fox hovering over her. "I was," Tamara drawled sarcastically. "What's up, Dr. Fox?"

Rodney was perched on the side of the sofa. "I need a place to crash for a while."

Tamara rose into a sitting position. She stared at the tall, slender pediatric orthopedist with curly red hair. Most of the staff referred to Dr. Rodney Fox as the brother with the red Afro. His soulful-looking brown eyes reminded her of a bloodhound.

"What's the matter?"

"Isis and I broke up and I need someplace to live until I find an apartment. Someone told me you have an extra bedroom. I'll pay whatever you want—just please don't say no, Tamara."

She closed her eyes again. Rodney and his oper-ating-room-nurse girlfriend had broken up and gotten back together so many times that their rela-tionship mirrored the antics of a TV sitcom. Tamara couldn't believe the brilliant young doctor just couldn't seem to get his love life together.

"Okay," she said, not opening her eyes. "You can stay as long as you want." Tamara held up a hand when Rodney leaned forward. "Don't you dare kiss me." He pulled back. "What time are you getting off?"

"Six."

She exhaled. "I'm hoping to get out of here at six. We'll leave together."

"Thank you, Tamara. You're an angel."

"Yeah, I know."

Tamara wanted to ask Rodney where her angel had been when she'd needed someplace to live after she'd left her husband. She'd checked into a less-than-desirable hotel until a rental agent had found her the two-bedroom apartment on East Seventh Street between Second and Third avenues. Although she only needed one bedroom, Tamara had decided to take it because living at the hotel was not an option.

The second and smaller of the two bedrooms remained empty for more than two years. It took her that long to save enough money to furnish and decorate the entire apartment. Tamara realized her monthly rent was twice what someone would pay for a mortgage for a house in the suburbs, but she had the luxury of not having to commute into the city.

She ran a hand over her hair. Rodney had disturbed her nap. "I'll see you later."

"Love you, Wolcott."

Tamara rolled her eyes at him. "Forget it, Fox. You're not my type."

He smiled. "Who is your type?"

"Not you," she countered.

She walked out of the lounge, replaying Rodney's query. Who was her type? The only name that came to mind was a man she'd met six hours ago.

Duncan Gilmore was her type. But was she his?

Chapter 3

It was six-thirty when Tamara took the elevator up to the surgical floor. She was tired but not a weary-to-the-bone fatigue. Maybe it was because she hadn't lost a patient. She wanted to return the keys to the anesthesiologist who'd let her use his apartment the afternoon before. She found him at the nurses' station with her supervisor, Brian Killeen.

Dr. Justin Luna smiled as she approached. "Have you recovered from yesterday's ordeal?"

Tamara returned his open, friendly smile. Justin Luna had become the hospital's rock star. Tall, dark, handsome and brilliant, he had successfully thwarted the advances of every woman at the hospital since he'd joined the medical staff the year before. What they didn't know was that Justin was engaged to marry an internist in his native Mexico City.

She handed him the keys to his co-op. "There was someone else with me in the elevator, so that kept me relatively calm."

Tamara nodded to her supervisor. His buzz-cut steel-gray hair was a match for his cold eyes. She'd managed to keep her distance from the tyrannical head of emergency services because a confrontation with him would signal the end of her career at the hospital. The first time he'd gotten in her face about the care of a patient was the only time. She'd handed in her resignation letter after applying for a position as an E.R. doctor at Beth Israel Medical Center and Lenox Hill Hospital. However, the chief of staff had intervened, forcing Tamara to reconsider her hasty decision. Two years had passed since that incident, and Doctors Killeen and Wolcott had kept a respectable distance and were overly polite with each other to the point of ridiculousness.

Brian Killeen's impassive expression didn't change with Tamara's greeting. "Dr. Luna, please excuse me for a moment. I'd like to have a few words with Dr. Wolcott." Cupping her elbow, he led Tamara away from the nurses' station.

She affected the same expression. "Yes, Dr. Killeen?"

He dropped his hand. "I wanted to tell you that I've approved your vacation request. I know you wanted it to begin Monday, but if you want to begin today, then you have my approval. I also wanted to tell you that a directive has come down from the corporation that we must cut back on overtime. Effective September first, we will no longer have twelve-hour shifts. We're now mandated to eight-hour shifts."

Tamara blinked once in an attempt to process what she'd just heard. The E.R. was the most under-staffed department in the hospital. With the faltering economy and loss of jobs, those who were no longer employed were left without health care, which tended to burden hospital emergency rooms with an increase in indigent patients.

"But that's going to put our patients at risk," she argued softly.

Brian stared at Dr. Tamara Wolcott. He may have come down hard on her, but he would be the first to admit that she was an excellent doctor. She'd never been one to complain. He'd found her to be one of the most dedicated doctors in the E.R.

"We're going to use residents and interns to pick up the slack. And I want you to think about becoming my assistant. You don't have to give me an answer until after you return from vacation."

The request shocked Tamara. She and Brian had never actually gotten along because of his bullying.

"Assist you how, Dr. Killeen?"

"I want you to supervise the interns."

"The only thing I'll say is that I'll think about it."

Thick black eyebrows lowered over his icy orbs. "What's there to think about, Tamara? Perhaps next year you'll become Head of Emergency Medicine."

Her eyes narrowed. "What aren't you telling me?" she whispered.

A rare smile softened the hard line of his mouth. "The only thing I'm going to say is that you should think about my offer." The smile vanished as quickly as it had appeared. "Because you're dressed in street clothes I assume you've completed your shift."

"I have."

"Then go home, Dr. Wolcott, I don't want to see you in this hospital for a month."

Stunned *and* shocked, Tamara blinked as if coming out of a trance. Not only had Brian called her Tamara for the first time and approved her four-week vacation request, but he'd also recommended her for a supervisory position. Although she was not suspicious by nature, she knew Dr. Brian Killeen hadn't told her everything. Perhaps, she mused, he'd been promised a position at another hospital. And if he had, then it was most likely Chief of Staff. There was no way *Dr. Blowhard*, as the E.R. staff called him out of earshot, would accept anything less than chief.

"I'll see you in a month." She was going to take him up on the offer to begin her vacation *now*. It'd been more than a year since she'd taken a day off for personal leave. Half the summer was over and Tamara planned to take advantage of the warm weather to do all of the things she'd put off doing.

Tamara turned on her heel and headed for the elevator that would take her to the lobby where Rodney had promised to wait for her. She found him leaning against the information desk talking to a volunteer. He straightened and followed her out into the early-morning sun.

Reaching for Tamara's hand, Rodney pulled her along as he whistled sharply through his teeth for a taxi that had just pulled up to the curb in front of the hospital. Opening the rear door, he waited for her to get in before he slid in beside her.

"East Seventh between Second and Third avenues," she said to the driver as he started the meter."

Rodney, wearing a baseball cap to protect his hair and face from the sun, placed a knapsack between his feet, then turned to stare at Tamara. "Have you ever walked from the hospital to your place?"

Tamara, who'd closed her eyes, nodded. "I've done it a few times. Most times I'm too exhausted to do anything but collapse when I get home."

"I don't know how you do it, Wolcott."

She opened her eyes, staring at his face. It was the color of a toasted pecan. Tamara had known Rodney

Fox for more than three years, yet this was the first time she actually looked closely at him, finding him quite nice on the eyes. His face was angular and on the thin side, but his features were delicately balanced. She'd told him that he wasn't her type, but then again he could've been her type if she hadn't put up a barrier to keep all men at a distance.

It had taken being trapped in an elevator with Duncan Gilmore for her to realize not all men were like Edward Bennett. Rodney's love life was like a soap opera—there was always drama before he and his girlfriend reconciled. What Tamara found odd was that Rodney had moved out of his *own* apartment, and she wondered if this break was final.

"Do what, Fox?"

"Work around the clock without falling on your face."

"You did it when you were on call."

"I know," Rodney said, "but that's when I was a resident. But as an E.R. physician you never catch a break."

Tamara smiled. "Give me a twenty-minute nap and I'm raring to go again. Working the E.R. is like a rush. I always find myself swept up in the chaos whenever a new patient is brought in."

"I can think of other things that give me a rush. Like sex," he added quickly when Tamara gave him a curious look.

She wanted to tell Rodney she didn't know about

that, because it'd been a long time since she'd had sex. The last man she'd slept with was her husband, and at thirty-six years her senior, his sex drive wasn't what it had been. This suited Tamara because it left more time for her to concentrate on her studies. Weeks would go by before they made love, and when they did she found it satisfying *and* also gratifying.

"You need more than sex," she countered.

"Without sex and babies the world wouldn't need pediatricians."

"You're right about that. You can put us out in the middle of the block," Tamara said to the cabbie, raising her voice to be heard through the Plexiglas partition.

Reaching into the pocket of his jeans, Rodney took out a bill and pushed it through the slot. "Keep the change." He opened the door, got out and helped Tamara. "I'm serious when I say that I'll pay half your rent."

Tamara stood on the sidewalk outside her apartment building staring up at Dr. Rodney Fox. "What about your co-op?"

"I'm putting it on the market. I told Isis she can live there until I find a buyer."

"That may take a while, given the real-estate market."

"True. But I'm not going to put her out on the street."

Unlike what Edward did to me, Tamara mused. Rodney deserved more than a woman who used him like a yo-yo. Unfortunately, Isis hadn't realized what she had. Hopefully she would come to her senses before it was too late.

"Come on, let's go upstairs. Let me warn you that you'll get your share of exercise walking up and down five flights. Most of the tenants are thirty- and fortysomething professional couples, which means you'll be able to sleep during the day. It is usually louder on the weekends, but it's never gotten so out of hand that the police have to get involved. The inner door is locked at all times, and thankfully there is a working intercom."

She unlocked the outer door, and walked into a vestibule with a number of mailboxes and an intercom system. "I'm in apartment 5F, which means I overlook the front of the building. The building superintendent is in 1F. His wife is our security," she said, lowering her voice to a whisper. "She sees everyone coming and going. Don't be surprised if she asks you what you're doing in the building."

Rodney smiled. "What do you want me to tell her?"

"You can say you're my cousin."

He angled his head. "We look nothing alike."

Opening her mailbox, Tamara removed a magazine and several pieces of junk mail. "Okay, Fox. We can be play cousins."

"Ain't that just like black folk?" he teased. "I think we're the only race with an abundance of play cousins."

Tamara laughed as she closed and locked the mailbox. "You're right about that."

Rodney followed her up the first flight of stairs. The smell of disinfectant lingered in the air. "The building is spotless."

"That's because Mr. Clifford sweeps the halls every day and mops every other day," she said over her shoulder. "There's a door at the end of the hall on the first floor that leads outside where you can put garbage. All garbage must be in plastic bags, or we'll have to pay a fifty-dollar fine for the first infraction. It escalates with each infraction. I'm thankful we don't have the dreaded New York City curse of roaches or rodents, and most tenants want to keep it that way."

"That sounds good to me."

Tamara reached the fifth floor and turned left down the tiled hallway. It had taken a month for her to get used to walking up the stairs. Not only was the exercise good for cardiovascular conditioning, but she'd also lost weight while toning her lower body.

She'd joined a local health club, but rarely worked out because she never seemed to find the time. However, with a month's vacation, she planned to visit the club several times each week.

Tamara remembered she'd told Duncan Gilmore that she had little or no time for socializing. But that was not the case now. She had a month—four weeks—to do whatever she wanted to do for herself. She planned to wait a few days, then call to tell him when they could get together for dinner.

She unlocked the door to her apartment and slipped out of her shoes. "Shoes worn at the hospital are left on what I call the quarantine mat." Tamara pointed to the mat under a table in the entryway. She opened a closet and took out a pair of flip-flops. "You can wear these." Rodney took off his cap and placed it on the table next to a bonsai plant. She gave him a pointed look. "You can always walk around in your bare feet, Fox."

Dropping his knapsack, Rodney slipped out of his running shoes, sat down on a straight-back chair with a seat made of rush and slipped on the rubber thongs. He stood up, towering over Tamara by a full head. "What are the house rules?"

Smiling, she stared at the shock of flyaway red curls falling over his forehead. "What makes you think there are any rules?"

His reddish eyebrows flickered. "You've already apprised me about the shoes and the garbage, so there have to be other rules."

"The only rule is that I'm not going to pick up after you. If you mess it up, then you clean it up. And you're toast if you touch or attempt to water my plants."

"That's easy," Rodney crooned.

"We will see," Tamara retorted.

* * *

Duncan lay on a cushioned chaise on the terrace outside his bedroom, bare feet crossed at the ankles. He'd taken a mental-health day.

The night before he and Kyle had gone over to Ivan's house after they'd closed their offices. They'd ordered takeout while watching the baseball game. He and Ivan had overruled Kyle, who didn't want to watch the Mets playing on the west coast, but after downing a few beers it didn't matter who was playing or on which coast. It was after three in the morning when he and Kyle had got into a taxi to return to their respective homes. The game had gone into extra innings.

Within minutes of walking into his bedroom, Duncan fell across the bed and went to sleep. When he woke the sun was up, and he'd called Mia Humphrey to tell her he wasn't coming in.

He wasn't hung over, but it felt good to lie around and do absolutely nothing. There were times when he felt guilty because Viola Gilmore had practically browbeat him by telling him he would amount to nothing if he didn't take advantage of every minute of the day. His aunt took him on what she'd called a field trip to several blighted neighborhoods to show him burned-out and boarded-up buildings, vagrants and drug addicts standing around aimlessly and men and women who carried all of their possessions with them and slept in doorways because they didn't have a place to call home. Viola equated laziness with failure, and even at fourteen, Duncan knew he didn't want to become a failure.

The ring of the telephone disturbed the quiet. Reaching over, he picked up the cordless without looking at the display. "Hello."

"Hel-lo."

He listened for the woman on the other end of the line to say something. "I think you have the wrong number," he said after the seconds ticked off.

"Is this Duncan Gilmore?"

Duncan sat up straighter, trying to remember where he'd heard her voice. "Yes, it is. Who's calling?"

"Hold up, playa. Don't you recognize my voice?"

"Tamara? Is that you?"

"Yes, it's Tamara. I…I didn't expect you to be home at this time."

"Is that why you called now? Because you were trying to avoid talking to me?"

A soft gasp came through the earpiece. "If I didn't want to talk to you, Duncan Gilmore, I never would've called. In fact, I would've thrown away your business card."

"But you didn't, and I'm glad you didn't."

"Why, Duncan?"

"Because I want to talk to you."

There came a pause. "What do you want to talk about?" Tamara asked.

"When are you available to have dinner with me?"

"I'm open, Duncan. Any day, any time."

A frown formed between his eyes. "Did you lose your job?"

"No," she said, laughing. "I'm on vacation."

He smiled. "If that's the case, then what are you doing tomorrow?"

There came another pause before Tamara said, "I have to check my calendar."

"I thought you said any time, any day."

"I did, Duncan. I was just teasing you."

"So," he crooned, "the doctor does have a sense of humor."

"Only when she's not working," Tamara retorted.

"How long are you on vacation, Tamara?"

"Four weeks."

Duncan whistled. "I suppose that's enough time for me to make you laugh."

"Hold up, numbers man. Don't get ahead of yourself. I only agreed to one date."

It was Duncan's turn to pause. "You're right. Forgive me for being presumptuous."

"You're forgiven, Duncan."

"Thank you. I have to make a reservation, then I'll call you back."

"Where are we going?"

"Sailing."

"Sailing?" Tamara repeated.

"Yes. I'd like to take you on a dinner cruise along the Hudson River. I can see the ship from where I'm sitting. We can eat, listen to music and, if you want, dance or just take in the view."

There came a beat. "That sounds wonderful."

"It should be fun. Give me your number and I'll call you back." Tamara recited her number, he repeated it to her. "Hang up, Tamara."

It took Duncan less than ten minutes to book a reservation. A satisfied smile softened his features when he dialed her number. She answered after the first ring. "I'll pick you up at six-thirty."

"What time do we board?" Tamara asked.

"Boarding is at seven-thirty and the cruise is from eight-thirty to eleven-thirty."

"What if I meet you at the pier instead of you coming down to get me?"

"No. I want to pick you up, Tamara."

"How will you get here?"

"I'll take a taxi."

"Don't. I'll take a taxi to you. Please give me your address."

Duncan knew insisting traveling downtown to pick up Tamara, only to have to return to Chelsea and walk three blocks to the pier would result in a verbal exchange, something he sought to avoid. He'd managed to make it through adolescence without a physical altercation because his mother and aunt preached constantly that it was better to walk away than confront.

He gave Tamara his address. "I'll be downstairs waiting for you."

"I'll see you tomorrow."

"Tomorrow," Duncan repeated, before ending the call.

He was going to share with Tamara Wolcott something he hadn't with Kalinda because she was prone to seasickness. Physically, Tamara was as different from his late fiancée as night was from day, but both possessed a quality he found hard to resist—the rare combination of brains *and* beauty.

Tamara sat at the breakfast bar in the kitchen pondering her decision after she'd hung up the phone with Duncan Gilmore. It had been four days since she'd found herself trapped in an elevator with the most delicious-looking man she'd seen in years. The only man who'd come close to Duncan was a boy in her high-school graduating class. His good looks had proved advantageous when he was picked by a modeling agency to be the poster boy for a men's cologne. His was the face of the nineties until drugs ravaged his looks and his career.

Although she'd never been turned on by a man's looks, Tamara found Duncan the exception. She'd considered the possibility that he was gay since he was single and hadn't fathered any children, then she chided herself for being biased and narrow-minded. If a woman chose not to marry or have children that did not necessarily make her a lesbian. When, she asked herself, had she become her mother? Moselle Wolcott was the most critical and opinionated woman on the planet, and Tamara feared she was no different when it came to Duncan Gilmore.

Resting her bare feet on the other tall high-back chair, she reached for the pen and pad and began making a list of things she had to do before her date. A trip to the hair salon was the first order of business, followed by shopping for an outfit suitable for a dinner cruise. It had been much too long since she'd had a date.

She'd dated a few men she'd met at several conferences, and she'd shared drinks with some of her male colleagues after her divorce, but she didn't count the latter as actual dates. They usually took place in a group after a particularly stressful shift. Otherwise she'd go over to a local restaurant or bar for late-night dinner, or, if it was the weekend, brunch.

Anytime she found a man getting too close she usually gave some signal that stopped them in their tracks. Duncan was geting too close, but was helpless to repel or discourage him. Perhaps it had something to do with them being trapped together, and not knowing when they'd be freed. Tamara also had told him things about herself that she hadn't revealed to her ex-husband because she thought she would never see or speak to Duncan Gilmore again. Oh, was she wrong. Not only had she spoken to him but she'd consented to see him again.

Tamara saw movement out of the corner of her eye and turned to find Rodney standing at the entrance to the kitchen. His damp hair was pasted against his scalp. He'd showered but hadn't shaved. The stubble of his beard was reddish blond. Rodney had moved in Tuesday morning and she'd only caught glimpses of him either when he came in early in the morning or left for his night shift.

She had turned her spare bedroom into a den with a sofa that converted into a queen-size bed. The walls were lined with bookcases, a flat-screen television with a home theater audio system, a mini fridge and a bar. It was a space where she went to relax and entertain. Whenever her parents came into Manhattan to see a Broadway show they had usually stayed overnight at a hotel until Tamara invited them to stay with her. The first time Moselle walked into the two-bedroom apartment she was at a loss for words because the space looked as if it'd been decorated for a design magazine.

Although Tamara spent more time at the hospital than she did at home, the apartment had become her sanctuary—a place where she was able to escape the stress that came with working as an E.R. doctor. She didn't own the apartment, but it was hers and hers alone. She invited who she wanted to her home and if she wanted solitude then she had the option of ignoring her phone or pager.

Smiling, she lowered her feet. "Good morning."

Running his hand over his flat belly under a black tank top, Rodney walked slowly into the kitchen and flopped down on the chair. He glanced up and stared at Tamara. "Is it?"

Her eyebrows lifted. "Rough night?" she asked.

Rodney covered his face with his hands. "I wish. I had a fight with Isis."

"I thought you broke up with her."

Lowering his hands, his tortured gaze fused with Tamara's. "She waited around for my shift to ask me if I'd mind if she brought a man back to the co-op."

"Isis is just jerking your chain, Rodney, because she knows she can get a reaction from you."

"It's over, Tamara. I gave her exactly one month to find a place to live, then I'm changing the locks."

Tamara didn't recognize the Rodney Fox sitting in her kitchen. His expression was cold and empty. She liked the normally affable doctor—a lot. He loved his patients, and they in turn loved him back. The first time she had worked with Dr. Fox was when a young boy was brought into the E.R. with a broken leg from a hit-and-run. Although the eight-year-old was in excruciating pain, Rodney had managed to make him smile. At that moment she realized he would make an incredible father.

Pushing back from the center island, she stood and went over to the sink. "Would you like coffee?"

"Yes, please."

"How do you drink it?"

"Black and strong."

Tamara reached for a cup and coffee disk, inserting it into the well of the coffeemaker. The smell of brewing coffee wafted in the space. "How about some breakfast, Fox?"

"Hanging out with you has its advantages. Perhaps I should've hit on you instead of Isis."

The brewing cycle completed, Tamara took the cup, placed it on a saucer and carried it to the table. "I don't think so," she drawled.

"Is it because I'm not your type?"

She patted his back. Baggy scrubs and street clothes had concealed Rodney Fox's lean, hard body. "I learned a long time ago not to mix business and pleasure. The results can be devastating."

Rodney took a sip of his coffee, peering at Tamara over the rim of the cup. "Are you speaking from experience?"

"Yes. I vowed not to get involved with anyone I have to work with."

"You know you've become an object of fascination at the hospital."

Tamara froze. "What are you talking about?" She knew she sounded defensive, but didn't care. She detested office gossip.

"I've lost count of the number of doctors who've come up to me to ask about you. They want to know if you're married," Rodney continued, "and if not whether you're seeing someone."

Waiting until her cup was filled with the aroma of coffee, Tamara carried it to the table and sat opposite her roommate. "What do you tell them?"

"I tell them to ask you."

Tamara smiled. "No one has ever asked me, so I assume they aren't *that* curious."

"That's because you're not only unapproachable, but also quite intimidating. No guy wants to be shot down before he can get close to you."

Her smile faded. "The one man I allowed to get close to me I married."

Rodney set down his cup, his hand shaking slightly. "You were married?"

"In a past life," Tamara confessed. "Are you going to bed or staying up for a while?" she asked, changing the topic. She didn't want to tell Rodney about her failed marriage because she wasn't certain whether he would repeat it, and she had no wish to become a part of the hospital rumor mill.

"I'm going to be up for a while. I'll probably crash later, but it won't matter because I'm off this weekend."

Tamara stood up. "Let's go out for breakfast. My treat."

Rodney rose to his feet. "Where are we going?"

"There's a coffee shop a couple of blocks from here."

"Would you mind if we go to my favorite diner? It'll be my treat."

She removed the cups from the table, rinsed them and placed them in the dishwasher. "Where is it?"

"Twenty-Second and Tenth."

Tamara felt her heart lurch. Rodney wanted to go to Duncan's neighborhood. In fact, that diner was only one block from where he lived. What, she mused, were the odds of her running into the man she planned to see the next day? She dismissed her musing, realizing she couldn't obsess over a man she hadn't known existed three days ago.

"Okay. As soon as I change my shoes I'll be ready to leave."

It had taken three days for her to get used to going to bed before midnight and not at sunrise, and for the next four weeks she would get up and go to bed, shop and take her meals like the average person.

Something else had changed for Tamara. For the first time in six months she would go out with a man—a man who intrigued her more than she wanted.

Chapter 4

Tamara forgot about running into Duncan when she sat in a booth at the Empire Diner with Rodney. It was the first time she'd eaten at the twenty-four-hour Chelsea eatery that was modeled after a black-and-white art-deco train car. She'd foregone her normal breakfast of cereal and fruit for steak and eggs.

She smiled across the table at Rodney. "This place is nice. I'm surprised I've never been here."

Rodney swallowed a mouthful of corned beef hash. "That's because you never venture beyond the East Side." He held up a hand. "Don't go off on me. You told me that yourself."

"I go to Macy's. And don't forget that I have to go to Penn Station to take the train to Long…"

Tamara's words trailed off when the last person she wanted to see at that moment walked into the diner. Although a battered baseball cap covered his head, and he had on a pair of sunglasses, a T-shirt, jeans and running shoes, she still recognized the tall man standing at the counter. He turned and looked in her direction for several seconds before cradling the bag a waiter had given him. She doubted that he'd recognized her in her painter's cap, peasant blouse and jeans. She exhaled an inaudible breath. He'd come to pick up a takeout order.

Rodney, realizing something had captured Tamara's attention, glanced over his shoulder. His gaze swung back to her. "Are you all right?"

She gave him a warm smile. "I thought I recognized someone I know." Picking up a glass, Tamara took a sip of water. "What's on your agenda for the weekend?" She'd segued from one topic to another smoothly and effortlessly.

"I have an appointment with a real estate agent later this afternoon to show the apartment. Tomorrow morning I'm going to Sag Harbor for the weekend. If you're not doing anything you can come along with me." Rodney's grandparents owned an oceanfront home in the exclusive enclave, and, as a child, he'd spent his summers there.

"Sorry, but I have something planned for

tomorrow evening." Tamara didn't want to tell
Rodney that she'd just seen her date for the following evening. "I'm not going back to the apartment
after we leave here," she told him instead. She
planned to go to Barneys, her favorite clothing shop,
to buy an outfit for the dinner cruise.

"Whatever you have planned I hope it's good,"
Rodney said with a wink.

"I'm certain it's going to be," she said confidently.

They finished breakfast and walked across
Twenty-Third to Fifth Avenue. Rodney decided to
walk back to the East Village while Tamara walked
another block to take the uptown bus.

Forty minutes after she'd walked into Barneys
she walked out with a dress and a pair of shoes. The
two items totaled a week's salary, but she hadn't
batted an eyelash because when she saw herself in
the mirror she realized she hadn't pampered herself
in a very long time. Lab coats and scrubs weren't
exactly haute couture.

She stopped in Saks to buy an evening bag,
perfume and makeup, feeling like a teenager on her
very first date. There was something about Duncan
that was different from the other men she'd known,
and Tamara knew it had nothing to do with his
looks. Besides, she didn't want to think of herself
as being *that* shallow. If she had been, then she
never would've married Edward. Not only was he
more than twice her age, but he wasn't what women

would call smokin' hot. He was what she referred to as charming and ruggedly attractive.

Duncan Gilmore, on the other hand, was so smokin' hot he sizzled!

Now the only thing she had to ascertain was whether he'd asked her out of a sense of chivalry or because he was as attracted to her as she was to him.

Duncan was waiting as the taxi pulled up to the curb. Walking around to the driver's side, he peered in to see the fare on the meter. Reaching into the pocket of his suit trousers, he took out a bill, handing it to the driver. "Keep the change."

He then opened the rear door to help Tamara. She placed her palm on his hand as he pulled her gently to her feet. Smiling, he turned her hand over and pressed a kiss to her scented wrist.

What Duncan saw rendered him speechless. Tamara had had her hair cut and styled into a profusion of curls that ended inches above her shoulders. The little black dress she wore was a silk sleeveless shift with a ruffled hem that flared around her knees. The four-inch heeled slingback pumps added several inches to her tall frame. He smiled when he saw the signature red soles. His gaze lingered on her expertly made-up face and her sensual mouth outlined in vermilion. The smoky colors on her eyelids made her eyes appear darker, mysterious.

"I didn't think you could improve on perfection,

yet you have," Duncan whispered reverently. Cupping her elbow, he leaned closer. "You even smell delicious."

Tamara lowered her gaze, totally unaware of the seductiveness of the gesture. "Thank you, Duncan." She glanced up, smiling. "You look wonderful—as usual." Sunlight slanted over his face, turning him into a statue of bronze. Again, she found herself transfixed by his large gold eyes.

A mysterious smile parted his lips. "What about yesterday?"

Her professionally waxed eyebrows lifted. "What about yesterday?" she asked, answering his question with her own.

"I know you recognized me at the Empire Diner yesterday."

"And you recognized me. Why didn't you come over and say something?"

"I didn't want to interrupt you and your *friend*."

Tamara smiled. "Why do you make *friend* sound like it's a bad word?"

Duncan inclined his head. "I didn't mean for it to sound like that."

"Rodney is a colleague."

"I'm glad I didn't interrupt you because you were probably discussing patients."

"I never talk about medicine or patients outside of the hospital. Once I end my shift, I divorce myself completely from whatever goes on in the

E.R. It's the only way I know to avoid burnout and maintain some distance from the patients who don't survive. I don't think I'll ever get used to calling a patient's TOD."

"You mean time of death?" Duncan asked.

"Yes."

"If that's the case, then we won't talk shop. I should've told you to come at seven, because it's going to be another hour before boarding begins. Would you mind hanging out at my place until it's time to leave?"

Tamara tilted her chin despite standing eye-to-eye with Duncan. "Of course I wouldn't mind." She glanced down the street. "This is really a charming neighborhood."

Releasing her elbow, he reached for her hand and led her to the entrance of a redbrick, four-story townhouse. "One of these days I'll show you the houses around the corner. Twenty to Twenty-First streets between Ninth and Tenth avenues have been designated a historic district. Do you know who Clement Clarke Moore was?"

"Didn't he write 'A Visit from St. Nicholas'?"

Duncan gave her fingers a gentle squeeze. "Well, well, well. Bright *and* beautiful," he crooned. "What a rare find."

Tamara ignored his compliment. "What about Clement Moore?"

"We have a park around the corner named for him."

She noticed Duncan said *we*. "He lived in Chelsea?"

"He gave the neighborhood its name. During the eighteenth century, the Moore house was considered a country estate. The family called it Chelsea. Professor Moore was also opposed to the abolition of slavery and owned several slaves during his lifetime."

"There's so much history in this city," Tamara remarked as she followed Duncan up the steps to the front door with stained-glass insets. Her eyes widened in amazement when he led her into a vestibule with exquisite nineteenth-century reproduction furniture.

"We'll take the elevator instead of the stairs."

Tamara smiled. "Are you certain you want to be in an elevator with me?"

Duncan dropped Tamara's hand, placing his in the small of her back and escorting her into the elevator. He slipped a key into the slot for the third floor. "I don't know about you, but I enjoyed being trapped in an elevator with you."

Tamara stared at the man standing several feet from her. He'd paired a claret-red silk tie and matching pocket square with a stark white shirt and a navy blue suit with a faint pinstripe. His black shoes were shiny enough for her to see her reflection.

"I have a confession to make."

Duncan held his breath, wondering whether

Tamara was going to tell him something he didn't want to hear. "What is it?"

"I'm claustrophobic. If you hadn't been in that elevator with me I probably would've succumbed to a panic attack. You kept me from losing it completely."

"Is that why you told me your life story?"

Pinpoints of heat stung Tamara's cheeks. "Easy, Duncan," she warned softly.

Throwing back his head, he laughed loudly. "I'm sorry about teasing you."

She rolled her eyes at him. "No, you're not."

"Yes, I am. Really," he added when she gave him a skeptical look.

The elevator door opened and the scene that greeted Tamara left her speechless. A spacious living room with a vaulted ceiling rising fifteen feet high was softly lit with recessed lights that reflected off bleached pine floors and a curving staircase leading to a loft. Six huge windows provided expansive views of the Hudson River and New Jersey.

Moving in a stiff, robotic motion, Tamara followed Duncan across the room, taking in the Venetian plastered walls and the leather-and-suede seating arrangement in neutral colors. A rectangular table with seating for eight, a matching sideboard and a beveled-glass breakfront in Honduran mahogany and inlaid rosewood were lit by a starburst designed chandelier. A magnificent gleaming black piano drew her attention.

"Do you play?" she asked Duncan who was staring at her with an amused expression.

"Yes. Do you?"

"Yes."

He angled his head. "One of these days we must play together."

Tamara wanted to tell him that he was getting ahead of himself. She'd only committed to one date and he was already talking about a second. "Do you mind if I try it? It's been years since I've played."

"Of course not," Duncan said, steering her over to the piano and pulling out the bench for her to sit.

Tamara placed her small evening bag on the bench and then rested her fingers on the keys to play a chord. A slow smile parted her lips when the harmonious notes floated upward and lingered. The acoustics were perfect.

She ran through the scales, her fingers moving at lightning speed. There had been a time when she had hated taking lessons and the endless hours of practice because the only music that interested her were the songs played on the radio or in music videos. Her Saturdays were filled with piano lessons, dance lessons and charm-school instructions. Her fingers stilled before she began playing a moving étude. Her hands never faltered when Duncan sat down beside her. She was lost in the music of her favorite composer, Chopin, the exquisite sound of a well-tuned instrument, the comfortably air-cooled space and the warmth she felt as the notes came back to her. Tamara lost track of time as she played the composition she'd memorized for her last musical recital. At fifteen she'd wanted to hang out at the mall with her friends, but Moselle had insisted she practice, practice and practice some more until she began dreaming that notes were attacking her. It was the first, but not the last, time she'd challenged her mother. She promised to practice, but the recital was to be her last. And it was.

Minutes passed as she finished the first and second movements, then she stopped, giving Duncan a sidelong glance. "I guess I got carried away. It's a beautiful instrument."

He angled his head and pressed a kiss to her thick fragrant hair. "That's because you play beautifully. I've never heard Chopin's Etudes de la Méthodes in F Minor played with such passion."

Tamara stared at him, complete surprise on her face. "You recognized the composer?"

"Yes, Tamara. Chopin is a favorite of mine."

She closed her eyes for several seconds. "I adore his work."

Duncan curbed the urge to kiss her hair again. "And it shows. Will you come back again so we can play together?"

"Of course I will. Where did you learn to play?"

His aunt had sacrificed a lot to give him piano lessons because she claimed playing an instrument would make him well-rounded. Even today, Duncan practiced the piano and continued his lessons with a retired professional virtuoso who'd played with several philharmonic orchestras and who lived around the corner.

A sad smile flitted across Duncan's face. "I'll tell you over dinner." Sliding off the bench, he held out his hand. "Come and I'll show you the rest of the house."

Tamara placed her hand in his, permitting him to ease her to her feet. Walking beside Duncan made her aware that wearing four-inch heels put her at eye-level with him, but he didn't seem to mind it. She'd known men who'd come onto her until she stood up. Standing five-ten in her bare feet, she knew she could be intimidating to some of them.

"How long have you lived here?" she asked Duncan when she walked into an ultra-modern, white-and-black kitchen.

A beat passed. "Almost ten years."

"How old were you when you moved in?"

"Twenty-nine."

"You're thirty-nine?"

Duncan hesitated before he said, "Yes. Why?"

Tamara smiled. "You look younger than that."

"How old do I look?"

"I thought you were in your early thirties. You must take good care of yourself."

"I try," Duncan said modestly. "You should see

my aunt. She just turned sixty-five and she could pass for someone fifteen years younger."

"There's no doubt you inherited good genes."

His expression changed as if someone had pulled down a shade to shut out the light behind his eyes. "I don't know about that. My mother died before her thirty-fifth birthday."

Tamara chided herself for the remark. "I'm sorry, Duncan."

"It's okay."

She wanted to tell him that it wasn't okay. Losing his mother at an early age probably had impacted his relationship with women. Tamara wondered about his father, but she already had asked him too many personal questions. Duncan was thirty-nine and he hadn't married or fathered children, and for Tamara that made him an ideal candidate for a relationship. He probably didn't want to marry, and neither did she.

However, she was ambivalent about motherhood. A part of her wanted to experience pregnancy, carrying a child to term, while another part of her was anxious and uncertain about whether she wanted to put her career on hold to be a stay-at-home mom until her child reached school age. Her sisters had delivered their children, then taken maternity leave and handed their infants over to live-in nannies.

Taking Tamara's hand, Duncan gave her fingers

a gentle squeeze. "Do you think I'm too young for you?" he teased, smiling.

"No, you didn't go there," Tamara whispered. "The only reason I married a man old enough to be my father was because I was dealing with a few childhood issues."

He took a step, bringing them only inches apart. "What about now, Tamara?"

"I've resolved most of them. And the few that remain aren't worth agonizing over. If I've learned anything in thirty-two years it's that there are things I can't control."

Tamara watched Duncan with a critical squint, wondering what was going on behind his golden orbs. Had she said something that had stirred up memories relegated to the recesses of his mind? The last thing she wanted was for the conversation to become uncomfortable. When she'd awakened earlier that morning, it was to a shiver of excitement she hadn't felt since she'd walked across the stage to receive her medical degree. Even when she'd exchanged vows with Edward she hadn't felt the nervous exuberance of a young bride. And later that night, after they'd consummated their marriage, she'd gotten out of bed and locked herself in the bathroom. She'd cried until she was spent, then washed her face and slipped into bed beside her snoring husband. Tamara had known then that she'd made a mistake, but she was resigned to making the best of it.

"Are you all right?" she asked him softly.

He flashed a practiced grin. "I'm wonderful, Tamara."

Duncan wanted to tell Tamara he'd spent more than half his life agonizing over what he couldn't control: losing his mother and his fiancée. The pain and grief had gnawed at him until he'd wanted to die, but his aunt's dedication to carrying out Melanie Gilmore's wish that her son make something of himself was stronger than his recurring bouts of guilt and self-pity.

He'd confessed to Ivan that he was ready to end one chapter in his life in order to begin another, and going out with Tamara Wolcott signaled that beginning. There was something about her that was special. She had a little extra something, different from the other women he'd known. The reason he'd asked her to have dinner with him was to figure out what it was.

Tamara turned her attention back to the white cabinetry, gleaming black appliances and granite counters. The black-and-white color scheme was repeated in the squares of the floor tiles. An assortment of pots, pans and utensils hung from a rack over a cooking island with double stainless-steel sinks.

"Did you do this kitchen over?"

"I had the entire loft renovated. The previous owner was an internationally known photographer who moved to London. What I like about this space is that it is a legal combination of three apartments. It still has two entries and two kitchens."

"Where's the other kitchen?"

"It's upstairs. There are two bedrooms on this floor, the living and dining room, a full bath off the kitchen and one in the larger of the bedrooms. I use the smaller room, which had been a maid's room, as my home office."

Tamara thought about her miniuscule two-bedroom apartment with a living room, eat-in kitchen and bathroom. "How many bedrooms are upstairs?"

"Two. Come upstairs with me."

She followed Duncan up the winding staircase to a catwalk running the width of the loft. "Are you a neat freak?"

He smiled. "No. Why?

"Everything is so clean."

"I have someone come in once a week. There was a time when I tried cleaning it myself, but I could never find the time to go through every room. By the time I dusted upstairs it was time to dust down-stairs. After a while I just gave up and called a maid service."

"How dirty can it get if you live here alone?"

He gave her a sheepish grin. "I don't know. I guess I never mastered the knack of housecleaning."

The black-and-white color scheme of the main-floor kitchen was repeated in the en suite bath upstairs. A claw-foot black tub sat on checkerboard tiles; placed on a diagonal, they enlarged the space. Large blocks of frosted glass provided a modicum of privacy for a corner shower stall.

Tamara was shocked at the size of the master bedroom. Both her bedrooms could easily fit into it. She averted her gaze from the California-king bed with chocolate-brown-leather head- and footboards. Everything in the room, from the massive armoire to the side tables, triple dresser and the small round table with two matching pull-up chairs was masculine.

Duncan drew back the wall-to-wall drapes to reveal a terrace spanning the width of the upstairs bedrooms. "This is where I hang out when I come home at night."

Tamara walked out onto the terrace. From where she stood she could see crowds coming and going at Chelsea Piers. "Even with the heat, there's still a breeze coming off the river."

Duncan found himself staring quietly as he gazed at the perfection of Tamara's long legs in heels and sheer black stockings. He hadn't lied to her when he'd told her that he didn't believe she could improve on perfection. Everything about her, from her curly hairdo to the soles of her designer pumps screamed sexiness personified. Now he knew why an older man would be attracted to someone less than half his age. Her ex-husband had seen something most men probably overlooked at first glance.

"The view is awesome."

He smiled. "That it is." Duncan wasn't talking about the view of the river. Taking several steps, he stood behind Tamara. "You're welcome to come back and enjoy the view whenever you want."

Glancing over her shoulder, Tamara met Duncan's eyes. He was serious. Duncan Gilmore wanted her to come back to his house and sit on the terrace outside his bedroom when he didn't even know how their first date would turn out.

"That would mean a second date."

"I know that, Tamara."

"Are you that certain there will be a second date?"

His impassive expression did not change. "I'm very certain."

She dropped her eyes before his steady gaze. "Are you always so confident, Duncan?" Her gaze returned to meet his.

"Confidence and success usually go hand-in-hand."

"I take it you're successful."

"I'm successful enough to get most of what I want."

Tamara couldn't believe his arrogance when she saw the direction of his gaze. He was looking at her breasts. But that gave her her answer about his sexual proclivity: Duncan Gilmore definitely wasn't gay.

"Careful," she warned in a soft voice. "Pride is a deadly sin."

"I don't think so," Duncan countered. "I was

taught that pride is a belief in one's own ability. Perhaps you're confusing pride with vanity, which I'm not."

Tamara wanted to tell Duncan he was deluding himself. He was vain. Even when trapped in an elevator with the temperature reaching dangerous levels he was still buttoned up to the throat.

Turning around to face him, she placed her hands on his shoulders, giving him air kisses on both cheeks. "Thanks for the offer." She smiled when his hands cradled her waist.

"Is that a yes?"

"Yes, it's a yes. Whenever I work a double shift I can come here to change my clothes and walk up three flights of stairs instead of getting stuck in an elevator in a highrise."

"Is that what you were doing when I saw you buttoning your shirt?"

"Yes, Duncan. One of my colleagues let me use his place to shower and change my clothes when I had to fill in for another doctor. You probably thought I was having an affair."

"The thought did cross my mind." When he'd walked into the elevator to find Tamara buttoning a man's shirt he'd thought she'd fled a lover's apartment to avoid a confrontation with the man's wife or girlfriend. Now that she'd explained the situation he was glad he was wrong. Duncan pressed a kiss to her forehead. "Let's head on

over to the pier. By the time we get there it will
be time to board."

They retraced their steps, and when Tamara
walked out into the warm evening air holding hands
with Duncan, she felt as if she'd known him forever.

Chapter 5

Tamara had accused Duncan of being proud and he'd denied it. But walking with Tamara and having men turn around to stare at her filled him with pride, pleasure and smugness that she was his—at least for four to five hours. To say she was stunning was an understatement. Her luxurious hair, beautiful face and statuesque body in the simple dress and designer stilettos were eyepopping and head-turning. He knew if he'd seen Tamara walking down the street she would've garnered his rapacious stare. He looped an arm around her waist when they stood in line waiting to board.

Tamara moved closer to Duncan's side, murmur-

ing, "The weather is perfect for an evening cruise."
A bright reddish-orange sun appeared to be suspended against a cloudless, cobalt-blue sky.

Duncan smiled. "You're right. And there's going to be a full moon tonight."

"That means the E.R. is going to jump tonight."

"Is it true that there are more E.R. visits during a full moon?"

"I've found it to be true, especially during warmer months. We definitely treat more stabbings and gunshot wounds. Child-abuse cases are more frequent during the colder months. Perhaps it has something to do with children being in the house for longer periods of time."

"I don't think I'd ever physically abuse my children."

Tamara heard a longing in Duncan's voice, wondering if there had been a time when he'd wanted to father children. "Remember, there isn't just physical abuse, Duncan. Some of the children seen in our psych unit come in with emotional scars that are far more devastating than physical ones. I see them as wounded little birds that will never soar with the other birds because they've retreated to a place where they feel safe."

"You probably should've specialized in psychiatry instead of emergency medicine."

"No, Duncan. I picked the right specialty for my temperament."

Attractive lines fanned out around Duncan's eyes when he smiled. "What about E.R. doctors?"

"We are adrenaline junkies always looking for that next rush. Even when I'm so exhausted and nearly falling asleep on my feet I get a rush of adrenaline whenever the emergency techs bring in another patient. Just the wail of a siren makes me shiver with excitement. However, the true test is to treat, heal and save every patient."

Duncan pressed his mouth to her ear. "You love being a doctor, don't you?"

Tamara felt his warm breath against her ear and cheek. Duncan was close, too close, but she wasn't going to ask him to move away. Whenever he took hold of her hand or rested his in the small of her back the gesture was executed with a naturalness that made her feel desired, protected.

She'd married Edward because she'd wanted him to love and protect her. She believed he did love her, but he'd loved gambling more. And he did protect her, but only from other men who expressed an interest in her. Once they saw the band of gold on her left hand most backed off.

"I love it more than anything else in the world."

Duncan wanted to ask Dr. Tamara Wolcott if she was willing to let something or someone else into her world. Would she permit herself to enjoy something other than practicing medicine? Was she willing to give him the opportunity to prove to her that all men weren't liars, duplicitous and untrustworthy?

Duncan liked Tamara. He wasn't certain whether it was because of her understated beauty, her intelligence or her sense of style, but what had shocked him was his offer for her to hang out at his condo. The last and only woman who'd been inside the duplex was Kalinda Douglas. As the only daughter of devoutly religious parents, Kali would come over to confer with the interior designer as to how she wanted to decorate the newly renovated space, to eat with him, to share a few moments of passion, then she would return to her Queens home where she lived with her parents.

He'd invited Tamara, but his intention was not to sleep with her. Unlike Kyle and Ivan, Duncan had never been a serial dater. His friends teased him about dating the same girl for long periods of time; however, the teasing had stopped when he revealed that he'd asked Kalinda to marry him. He would've been the first of the trio to marry if not for an unforeseen disaster. Now he would stand as best man for Kyle when he married Ava Warrick.

The line began moving as chicly attired men and women boarded the sleek all-glass dining vessel. The *Celestial* was an elegant ship designed for comfort and stunning views. The passengers were greeted by a trio of musicians playing a baby grand piano, an acoustic bass and a classical guitar who set the mood with a sophisticated jazz composition. Duncan and Tamara shared a smile before they were shown to their table for two. A stark white table-cloth, a bud vase with a fresh rose and an unob-scured view through glass walls and ceiling set the stage for a night of luxurious, intimate, romantic dining.

Tamara stared at Duncan across the small expanse separating them. Everything about him conveyed elegance and breeding, and he appeared so sure of himself and his place in the world.

A hint of a smile tilted the corners of his mouth. "What are you thinking about?"

"How much I'm enjoying hanging out with you."

Reaching over the table, Duncan grasped her hands, examining the manicured nails painted a pale beige. Her hands, though delicately formed, were those of doctor, a healer. "If you're open to it, then we can have a lot of fun together."

She blinked once. "Are you talking about a rela-tionship, Duncan?"

"No. I'm talking about friendship, Tamara. A re-lationship means a physical involvement, and I'm not going to presume you'd want to sleep with me."

Tamara leaned closer. "Do you sleep with women?"

Duncan, taken aback by her query, recoiled. "Of course I sleep with women. Did you think I was gay?" he whispered, visibly perturbed.

"I'd thought about it," she said truthfully.

"Why, Tamara? Because I wasn't all over you?"

Heat suffused her face as she averted her gaze. Duncan had tightened his grip on her fingers when she stared at him again. "I thought it strange that you'd ask me to go out with you when you could get any woman you want because of the way you look. And then, when you told me you weren't married, didn't have a girlfriend or children, I presumed perhaps you weren't into women."

"You presumed wrong."

"I know that now."

"I like women, Tamara. In fact, I like them a lot." His eyes narrowed. "Why do you look so disappointed?" A beat passed. "Were you hoping I wasn't heterosexual?"

"Yes and no. Yes, because whenever I sleep with a man it eventually spoils everything. And no, because if or when you decide to marry, you will make some woman a wonderful husband."

"You sound very sure about that."

Tamara smiled, causing his gaze to linger on her lush mouth. "I work in a male-dominated profession, Duncan, and that means I get to interact with a lot of them on a daily basis. I've become quite astute in differentiating the good ones from the dogs, and I've met more than my share of woof-woofs. Titles like doctor don't make them exempt. Edward was a prime example of that."

"Thankfully, he's out of your life."

"I'll definitely drink to that."

Duncan let go of Tamara's hands. "Speaking of drinks, will you share a bottle of wine with me?"

"Yes, I'd love to."

It was close to nine o'clock when the ship pulled away from the pier. It was filled nearly to capacity with couples and small groups enjoying the music of the trio serenading them with jazz, blues and classical favorites. The entertainment was a perfect complement to sipping fine wine while enjoying exquisitely prepared gourmet cuisine.

Tamara didn't know which she enjoyed more: the sight of the greatest skyline in the world, the food or her dining partner. Duncan had ordered a bottle of pinot grigio to go with their appetizers of seafood bisque and herb chevre parfait and entrées of miso-glazed wild Alaskan salmon and free-range Tuscan chicken breast.

The sun had set and a full moon illuminated the shore as the Empire State Building and World Trade Center site were shrouded in darkness. After dinner there was a short break in the entertainment, and when the trio returned they were accompanied by a singer who stopped by each table, cabaret-style, singing Broadway and popular hits.

Couples were up crowding the ample dance floor, moving to upbeat dance music that spanned big-band, Motown and pop favorites. Duncan stood up, came around the table and eased Tamara to her feet. He led her out to the outdoor deck near the bow, took her into his arms and pressed his cheek to hers as the vocalist launched into the Luther Vandross hit, "Here and Now."

The cool night air swept over Tamara's exposed skin, bringing with it a shiver that had nothing to do with the weather. Being in Duncan's embrace, her body molded to his, felt so right. The area between her thighs throbbed with a need she'd forgotten.

Tamara's sexual war with her ex-husband had not punished him but herself. Tamara had convinced herself that she didn't want a man, didn't need one, but dancing with Duncan Gilmore proved her wrong. He felt good and smelled incredibly masculine as he spun her around and around on the open deck.

All too soon the song ended and she loathed having to go inside. "Can we stay out here for a little while?"

Duncan smiled as he kissed her earlobe. Tamara hadn't worn any jewelry except for pearl studs. "Of course we can."

She turned to stare out over the bow, smiling when Duncan wrapped his arms around her waist. She managed to stifle a gasp when she felt the throbbing hardness against her buttocks. It was obvious their dancing together had aroused him as much as it had her.

The light from a full moon lit up the sky as the ship neared the Brooklyn Bridge. Tamara stared at what she regarded as one of the greatest engineering feats of all time. A light breeze lifted the curls framing her face.

"You promised that you'd tell me about yourself."

Duncan registered a breathless quality in Tamara's voice. He didn't want to talk but just to enjoy the feel of her ripe body pressed to his. He knew she was aware of his arousal, but he wasn't about to apologize for something he couldn't control.

"What do you want to know?"

She smiled. "Anything you're willing to divulge."

"You make it sound as if I've been living a double life."

"We all have secrets, Duncan."

"That's true, but I have nothing to hide. I'm an only child. My mother dropped out of college in her sophomore year when she found out she was pregnant. She'd met this guy who wasn't a student, slept with him once and her life changed forever. When she went looking for him to tell him she was carrying his child, she couldn't find him."

"Where did she go to school?" Tamara asked.

"It was a small college in western New York. She returned home and told my grandmother that she was going to have a baby, and all hell broke loose. There was so much hostility between my mother and her widowed mother that Mom moved out to stay in a facility for unwed mothers. A social worker got her on social services and found her an apartment in public housing. Mom waited until I was a year old, then applied for a job in a bank."

"Who took care of you while she worked?"

"She paid the next-door neighbor to look after me. Meanwhile she saved what she could from her meager paycheck and went back to school. It took her several years, but she eventually graduated from the American Institute of Banking with a degree in financial management. She was promoted to a junior officer. Her plan was to save enough money to put down on a house in the suburbs, but her dream never materialized."

"What happened, Duncan?" Tamara asked after a long silence.

"She died of a blot clot. I should've known something wasn't right because Mom had begun complaining about chest pains. She said she had troubling breathing, but said it was probably indigestion because she always had a sensitive digestive system. One morning it got so bad that she called in sick. I went to school, and when I came home I found her on the kitchen floor. A neighbor called the police and when the emergency technicians got there they said she'd been dead for hours. I blamed myself because I should've insisted she see a doctor."

Tamara turned around, her hands cradling his face. "Don't beat up on yourself. You were just a kid."

Duncan closed his eyes. "A kid who knew there was something wrong with his mother."

"What could you have done, Duncan? If you'd told her to see a doctor, would she have done it? I'm a doctor and I've lost count of the number of times I've told my patients that they must take their medication, or that they should follow up on my recommendation to see a specialist, but invariably they end up in the E.R. again and again. It took me a while to realize that people control their own destinies."

"My grandmother had passed away, so social workers were going to send me to a group home until my aunt stepped in and requested legal guardianship. She was seven years older than my mother and had become a schoolteacher. Aunt Viola taught in Brooklyn where she'd rented a two-bedroom apartment in a Brooklyn Heights brownstone. Years later she bought the building from the owners, who relocated to Florida.

"Aunt Viola stressed education until it was coming out of my ears. I got into Brooklyn Tech and earned the reputation of being a nerd. I had the glasses and read lots of books and when I ventured into some of the rougher neighborhoods I realized I had to assume a different persona or get my butt kicked."

Lowering her hands, Tamara put her arms around his neck. "Somehow I can't see you as a nerd."

"You wouldn't say that if I take out the contacts and wear my glasses."

Duncan's disclosure surprised Tamara because she didn't know that he wore contact lenses. "Don't nerds wear high-water pants and pocket protectors?"

Smiling, Duncan shook his head. "Those are stereotypical nerds. I can assure you that I'm more nerd than playa. My mother wouldn't let me hang out with the kids in the projects because some of them were cutting classes, getting into drugs and becoming fathers. I was allowed to play with two boys in my building. Kyle Chatham, Ivan Campbell and I were inseparable. The year we turned thirteen we became blood brothers. We made a pact not to get into drugs, not to become what today would be called baby daddies, to graduate from college and to buy a brownstone."

"Did it happen, Duncan?"

"Yes. We hung out in one another's apartments studying instead of on the corner. Kyle went on to become a lawyer and Ivan became a psychotherapist. Even though I moved to Brooklyn I managed to keep up with my friends. We'd meet in the Village or Times Square. A few times they came to Brooklyn and we'd hang out at Coney Island."

"Did you all go to the same college?"

"No. Kyle graduated from John Jay College of Criminal Justice with a degree in pre-law. I went to Baruch College and Ivan went to NYU and was a psychology major. I interned at a public accounting firm to prepare for the CPA exam. I passed and then went to work for an investment company while attending Pace University for my MBA. I just applied to a joint JD/MBA degree program."

"Why get another MBA?"

"I have an MBA in finance, but if I get into the JD/MBA program, then I can specialize in portfolio management and focus on developing venture capital funds that invest in local communities."

"Do you plan to practice law?"

"Not in the traditional sense. The goal of the program is to closely integrate a course of study in both fields. When I successfully complete the program I'll also have a law degree."

"Have you taken the LSAT?"

He nodded. "Yes."

"Did you pass?" Tamara teased.

Duncan nodded again. "Yes. I've applied for a waiver to audit the business contracts courses I've already taken."

"Do you think you'll get approval?"

"I'm hoping I will because I've already earned an MBA from Pace."

"How many credits do you need to complete both programs?"

Duncan's eyes narrowed when he added the numbers in his head. "It will be a total of one hundred twenty-three—eighty from the law school and forty-three from the business school."

"That's going to take you at least four years—that's if you go full-time."

"I plan to go part-time, because I still have a business to run. It'll take six years, but I have nothing but time. I'll attend law school for two years and the business school for one, then take courses in both schools for three years. I can always accelerate by attending summer sessions."

Duncan told her that he'd worked for a major investment company, making millions for their clients while building his own portfolio. He'd made a small fortune when tech stocks boomed, and then sold them before the stock price tumbled. He'd bought the loft, had it renovated and moved from Brooklyn to Manhattan. Ivan had returned to New York after living and working in D.C., and had talked him into purchasing a foreclosed brownstone together.

"Ivan decided to set up a practice in Harlem and asked me if I was tired of making rich people richer. I took that to mean that I should concentrate on people in our own community. It took me less than a month to take him up on his offer. I told him to contact the real estate broker. We hadn't gone to contract when I approached Kyle to ask him whether he wanted to go in with us. I'd put together an investment portfolio for Kyle, so I knew he had enough liquidity even though he'd purchased his own brownstone on Strivers' Row. He didn't hesitate, because he'd been complaining about working eighty-hour weeks for a Park Avenue law firm. Once the renovations were completed I left Wall Street. Kyle eventually resigned from the law firm, and the childhood dream of owning a Harlem brownstone became a reality."

Tamara admired Duncan. He knew exactly what he wanted for his future, while she wasn't certain whether she would accept Dr. Killeen's offer. She'd gone into medicine to provide the best care for her patients, not to become an administrator. Administrators ran hospitals. Doctors provided patient care.

She leaned closer. "Did anyone ever tell you that you are awesome?"

Cradling her waist, Duncan eased her to stand between his outstretched legs. "No."

"Well, you are, Mr. Gilmore."

Duncan flashed a sheepish grin. "Why thank you, Dr. Wolcott."

Tamara knew he was going to kiss her, and she wanted him to. Duncan's mouth covered hers in a gentle joining that heated her blood to the point of scalding.

It didn't matter that she hadn't known him a week, or that this was only the second time they'd come face-to-face. What mattered was the dizzying rush of desire that reminded her that she'd denied the strong passion within her for much too long. A soft moan of ecstasy slipped through her lips when Duncan deepened the kiss.

Tamara desperately needed more than a kiss. She wanted to feel flesh against flesh, she wanted him inside her.

"Duncan," she whispered, struggling to breathe. "Take me back to the table." She had to put some distance between them or embarrass herself by begging him to take her back to his loft and make love to her.

Duncan had planned to kiss Tamara, but he wasn't prepared for the sense of urgency that made him want to strip her naked and make love to her under the light of the full moon. "I'm sorry."

Tamara stared at Duncan. "I hope you're not apologizing for kissing me?"

"No. I'm apologizing for not asking whether I could kiss you."

She waved a hand. "It's all right, Duncan. It was only a kiss."

It was only a kiss. Her rejoinder echoed in Duncan's head as he escorted Tamara back to their table. He'd practically embarrassed himself because his body refused to follow the dictates of his brain, and her glib comeback that it was only a kiss was like covering a gash with a Band-Aid.

He pulled out her chair for her, then sat down himself. Grabbing the wine bottle, Duncan refilled his glass. Touching his glass to her half-filled one, he inclined his head. "I toast our first kiss."

Tamara picked up her glass, holding it aloft. "And I hope it won't be the last."

Duncan wondered if Tamara was into playing head games, because if she was then this first date would become their last date. "What's up with you? You want me to bring you back to the table, then you tell me that you want me to kiss you again. What gives?"

Tamara's eyes narrowed with her rising temper. "Do you know how long it's been since I've been kissed?" She'd practically spat out the last word. "It's been eight months, Duncan," she continued. "The last time a man kissed me was on New Year's Eve. He had a comb-over, bad breath and was old enough to be my grandfather—everything you're not, and you expect me not to be affected by your kiss? I asked you to bring me back to the table because it's safer here than out on deck."

"Safer for who?" he asked, so softly Tamara had to strain her ears to hear his query.

"It's safer for me, because being alone with you reminds me of what I've been denied."

He blinked once. "And what's that?"

A sad smile pulled down one side of her mouth. "That I am a woman, that I enjoy being kissed and that it's all right to feel passion and desire."

Putting the wineglass to his mouth, Duncan took a deep swallow, then set it on the table. "If that's the case then I'll make certain to kiss you again and again and again."

Smiling, Tamara drained her glass and held it out to be refilled. She and Duncan stared at each other, seeming to read each other's thoughts, until the vocalist approached their table, asking if they had a special request.

Duncan glanced around to find dozens of eyes watching him and Tamara. He said the first song that came to mind, "The Closer I Get to You."

"Excellent choice," she crooned. Raising her microphone, she nodded to the pianist. "This beautiful couple has requested 'The Closer I Get to You.' All those who want to get closer to that special person this is your chance to get up and dance."

All around them men and women were rising and filling the dance floor. Duncan pushed back his chair and came around to Tamara. She rose gracefully and went into his embrace, and they joined the other couples. The illuminated Statue of Liberty monument came into view as Tamara lost herself in the magic of the night and the pull of the man holding her to his heart.

The magic continued as Tamara lay in Duncan's protective embrace in the back of the taxi speeding recklessly across town to the East Village. Her first date with him had been nothing short of perfection. The musical entertainment had topped off an evening of exceptional food and wine, spectacular skyline views and a sophisticated crowd that had come to enjoy themselves. Many of the passengers had been celebrating birthdays and anniversaries. Two couples had gotten engaged during the cruise, eliciting shrieks of surprise and joy. The taxi driver pulled up to the curb in front of Tamara's apartment building. She waited until Duncan settled the fare. He got out and pulled her effortlessly to her feet.

Opening her tiny evening purse, she took out her keys. The curtain at the window on the first floor stirred. "That's the wife of the building superintendent," she whispered. "She's the building's unofficial security."

"She's only protecting her neighbors."

Tamara opened the inner door and headed for the staircase. "I live on the fifth floor."

Duncan remembered Tamara telling him she lived in an overpriced Village walkup. All of Manhattan was overpriced and that included his neighborhood.

He followed her up the stairs. "There's no doubt you get your cardio workout every time you walk up." His gaze lingered on the shape of her legs in the stilettos. Duncan had always thought himself a breast man, but looking at Tamara's long, sexy legs had him debating which he liked best.

He made it to the fifth floor without breathing heavily. He took the key from Tamara, unlocked the door to her apartment and was greeted with cool air and light from a table lamp in the small foyer. Lush green plants in colorfully painted pots lined the length of the rustic table.

Tamara slipped out of her shoes and left them on the mat under the table. She had to look up at Duncan for the first time that evening. "Thank you for a wonderful evening."

Duncan placed her keys on the table next to her evening bag. "You made it wonderful, Tamara."

She smiled up at him. "Now, that's debatable, Duncan."

Cupping the back of her neck, he pulled her closer and slanted his mouth over hers, swallowing her breath when her lips parted. "Does this mean we can do it again?" he whispered.

"Yes."

Pulling back, Duncan stared at the black slanting eyes in a flawless tawny-brown face. He hadn't wanted the night to end, but knowing Tamara had agreed to go out with him again had tempered his patience. "Good night."

She smiled. "Good night."

Duncan was there, standing in her foyer, and then he was gone, Tamara closing and locking the door behind him. She went into the living room and parted the blinds with a finger, peering down at the street below. Minutes later she saw Duncan as he walked to the corner to flag down a taxi. She was still standing in the same position when he got into one and it sped away.

He's a winner, she mused.

She'd been given a second chance. Not only was Tamara older this time, but she was also wiser, wise enough not to get in too deep and wise enough to recognize when it was time to get out.

Chapter 6

Duncan walked down the block to the brownstone that had become his home after Melanie Gilmore passed away. He'd promised his aunt that he would come for dinner Sunday, but had made a stop at Junior's restaurant to pick up Viola's favorite dessert—strawberry cheesecake.

What he found odd was that he'd had Sunday dinner with Viola the week before. They'd agreed to get together twice a month during the school year, and once during the months of July and August. Either he went to Brooklyn or she came to Manhattan.

Viola planned to retire at the end of the upcoming

school year. She'd given New York City school children forty-four years of her life—the last twenty as principal and assistant principal. When Duncan asked his aunt she what she'd planned to do after she retired, her response was "travel, travel and travel some more."

What he couldn't understand was that she'd always traveled. She'd taken him with her on an extended tour of Ireland and the British Isles the year he celebrated his fifteenth birthday. He could look forward to visiting the Caribbean during the Christmas recess, other states during spring break and Europe, Africa or Asia in the summer. By the time he'd entered college Duncan had lost count of the number of countries, islands and states he'd seen.

Traveling with Viola had come with a proviso— he had to maintain a ninety average or he would be left with a distant cousin who owned a North Carolina hog farm. It'd taken one trip to the hog farm to turn him off. It was another three years before he could eat bacon, ham or ribs without seeing the beady eyes or snouts. He still couldn't bring himself to eat pigs' feet or chitterlings.

Duncan bounded up the steps of the brownstone. Reaching into the pocket of his jeans, he took out a key and opened the solid-oak door adorned with a colorful wreath of dried summer flowers.

Viola used the street level of the three-story building for entertaining, the first floor for her personal quarters and she'd rented out the apartments on the second and third floors. Once Duncan had graduated from college and gotten a job, he'd rented one of the apartments on the top floor.

As soon as he stepped into the vestibule a distinctive nauseating odor wafted into his nostrils. He frowned and was still frowning when he rang the bell before unlocking the door to his aunt's apartment. She met him as he closed the door.

"Did I smell crack in the vestibule?"

Viola Duncan nodded as she stared up at her nephew. He was dressed for the off-and-on drizzle that had begun at dawn. Today he wore a baseball cap, jeans, a rugby shirt, a lightweight jacket and running shoes. He'd replaced his contact lenses with a pair of black wire-rimmed glasses.

"That's why I wanted you to come over. I'd suspected Mr. Hughes was smoking something, but I can't identify what it is. I know for certain it's not marijuana." Philip Hughes had rented the second-floor apartment overlooking the front of the house.

Duncan leaned over and kissed his aunt's cheek. With the exception of his height, he and Viola looked enough alike to be mother and son. Her curly hair was salt-and-pepper and her khaki-colored skin showed no signs of aging. A few lines fanned out around her eyes, but only when she smiled.

Viola had been engaged to a lawyer when she became her nephew's legal guardian, but it was years later when Duncan learned that his aunt ended the engagement because her fiancé was opposed to starting marriage with a ready-made family. He had resented having to compete with a teenage boy for his wife's attention. And because Viola had sacrificed her happiness for him, there wasn't anything Duncan wouldn't do for her.

"Where is he?"

Viola heard something in her nephew's voice that sent a shiver over her body. "He's upstairs."

Duncan placed the box with the cake on a side table and removed his cap and jacket, hanging them on a wooden coat rack. "I'm going upstairs to have a chat with him."

Before renting any of the units, Duncan had taken on the responsibility of interviewing prospective tenants and running their credit history. The tenant Viola was complaining about was a high-school science teacher.

Viola adjusted her rimless glasses, large light-brown eyes filling with concern. "Don't go up yet, son."

A slight frown creased his forehead. "What aren't you telling me, Aunt Vi?" It was on very rare occasions that his aunt referred to him as her son. Most times it was when she was anxious.

"I asked him if he was smoking in his room, and he told me to mind my business. I had to remind him that there is a no-smoking clause in his lease."

"What did he say to that?"

"He told me to, and I quote, 'kiss my ass,' end quote. No, Duncan!" she screamed when he turned and walked out of the living room. "I spoke to Kyle's friend Micah about it."

Duncan stopped his retreat, turning to face Viola. "What did he say, Aunt Vi?"

"Micah said to call him when you got here. He got a judge to sign off on a warrant, and his next-door neighbor, who is a police officer, is willing to serve it. Tessa also invited us to share dinner with them."

Micah Sanborn and his wife Tessa lived in the same close-knit Brooklyn Heights neighborhood as his aunt. Kyle had told him that wedding planner Tessa Whitfield-Sanborn had agreed to coordinate the Warrick–Chatham nuptials.

Taking out his cell phone, Duncan scrolled through his address book and punched in the number for Micah's home number. Micah answered on the second ring. "Where are you, Duncan?"

"I'm in my aunt's living room."

"Stay there. Jack Cleary and I will be over in about ten minutes."

Duncan ended the call, then escorted his aunt into the kitchen to wait for the Kings County ADA and his neighbor the police officer to arrive. If it'd been up to him Duncan would have barged into the apartment and snatched the man up by the throat for disrespecting his aunt. But he knew how much Viola detested violence, so he would take Micah's advice and wait.

"Sit down, Duncan," Viola said, watching Duncan pace the length of the large kitchen.

He stopping pacing and sat on a high stool at the cooking island. "This will be the last day Philip Hughes will spend under this roof."

Viola busied herself, putting up a kettle of water to make tea. "Do you want tea, Duncan?"

"No, thank you."

"How have you been, son?"

Duncan smiled for the first time. "I'm good, Aunt Vi."

She gave him a sidelong glance, silently admiring his tall, graceful body. Viola Gilmore couldn't have been more proud of Duncan if he'd actually been her son. Although a single mother, her sister had done a remarkable job during his formative years. Melanie had given him a good foundation and Viola had improved on it.

There were times when she knew she was being too preachy about him working up to his intellectual potential, avoiding gangs and physical confrontations, not abusing alcohol or drugs and always using protection when having sex, but it had worked. Duncan had far exceeded her expectations.

"Have you met someone?"

Duncan angled his head, his expression one of faint amusement. "Yes, I have."

With wide eyes, Viola stared at him. "You have?"

"Yes, I have," he repeated.

"Do you mind if I ask how you met her?"

"We got stuck in an elevator together. I asked her out and she accepted."

Viola approached her nephew and hugged him. "I'm so happy for you, Duncan. You don't know how long I've been praying for you to meet someone so I can become a grandmother."

"We've only had one date, Aunt Vi."

"How was it?"

"Good," Duncan confirmed.

"You can call me a nosy old woman, but I'm going to interrogate you anyway. Are you going to see her again?"

Duncan gave his aunt a long, penetrating look. Either he'd changed or she had, because in the past they had never talked about the women he'd dated. He'd been very discreet when he'd invited any to spend the night with him, always cognizant that although he was paying rent he still lived under his aunt's roof.

"I plan to, Aunt Vi."

Viola dropped her arms when the kettle began whistling. "You know that I worry about you being alone."

Duncan kissed her hair. "That's what mothers are supposed to do."

Her eyes glistening with moisture, she went to

turn off the stove. "God sent you to me because he knew I would never have children of my own."

"I've thought about adopting a child."

Viola's hand shook slightly as she attempted to fill a cup with hot water. "Are you serious?"

"Of course I'm serious. I shouldn't have to tell you about the number of children of color languishing in foster care because no one wants to adopt an older child. I have more than enough room in my home and I meet the income criteria."

"But a child should have two parents."

"I grew up with a single aunt and mother and I turned out all right."

"You were the exception, Duncan."

"And my son would also become the exception."

Reaching for a bottle of honey, Viola added a spoonful to the steaming tea. This was a side of her nephew she'd never seen before. When he'd lost his fiancée he'd sworn never to marry or father children. Now he was talking about adopting a child.

Viola knew any child Duncan adopted would have a wonderful role model for a father. There was no doubt he would stress education, take him to sporting events and expose him to the arts. The first time she'd taken Duncan to a ballet it was to see *The Nutcracker* at Lincoln Center. Her nephew was more enraptured by the music than the costumes and dancing because he was familiar with the works of Tchaikovsky. She stopped stirring the tea when the sound of the doorbell echoed throughout the apartment.

Duncan moved off the stool. "I'll get it."

He walked to the door and opened it. Micah and another man wearing street clothes stood on the steps. He shook hands with the assistant district attorney. "Thanks for coming."

Micah smiled, even though the warmth didn't reach his dark, deep-set eyes. Tall, dark, with even features, the former NYPD lieutenant had made a name for himself as a tough prosecutor for the district attorney's "gang busters" division. He'd prosecuted several gang members who were now serving lengthy sentences in state prisons.

"Duncan, this is Jackson Cleary. I brought him along as backup."

Duncan offered his hand to the police officer. "I appreciate your help, because otherwise you'd have to arrest me for kicking this dude's ass for disrespecting my aunt."

Jackson's blue eyes narrowed. "I'll kick his ass for you."

As if on cue, Jackson and Micah reached into the pockets of their jeans for small leather cases with their badges. Micah nodded to Duncan. "You go up and see if he'll open the door for you. If he doesn't, then Jack and I will take it from there."

Duncan led the way to the second floor. He knocked on the door to Philip Hughes's apartment, listening for movement. The smell of crack was even more pungent.

"Who is it?" The query came out slurred.

"Duncan Gilmore. Open the door, Mr. Hughes. I'd like to talk to you."

"Get the hell outta here and leave me alone!"

Duncan tried the knob. The door was locked. "It's all yours," Duncan said to the police officer. He stepped back when Jackson Cleary pounded on the solid-oak door.

"Mr. Hughes, this is the police. I want you to open the door."

"Not without a warrant."

Jackson winked at Micah. "I just happen to have one, Mr. Hughes. Now open the door."

There came the sound of shuffling feet before the click of the lock opening. The door opened and Duncan stared numbly at the man. He hardly recognized him. He was thin, almost to the point of emaciation. His normally shaved brown pate bore stubble. The haze clouding the room had an acrid smell. Jackson slapped the warrant against the man's frail chest.

"Go sit down before you fall down."

Duncan stood off to the side as Jackson began his search. A table was littered with dozens of tiny pellets, glassine packets filled with white powder and what appeared to be marijuana. A crack pipe lay nearby.

"Hey, Sandy, you need to take a look at this." Jackson was staring at a computer monitor.

Micah walked over to see what his old police-academy buddy was looking at. He smothered an expletive when he saw the shocking images, they threatened to make him physically ill. "Cuff the freaky bastard and read him his rights. Then call someone from the Sex Crimes Unit to pick up this computer. Make certain they search the apartment for more tapes or disks."

Duncan had an idea of what was on Philip Hughes's computer screen. He motioned to Micah to step out into the hall. "Try to make this as unobtrusive as possible for my aunt."

Micah nodded. "I'll make certain they send an unmarked car. He's going to be charged with drug possession and child pornography. I'm going to make certain he'll never set foot in a classroom again. Why don't you take your aunt over to my place? Give me your keys and I'll lock up the place. Tell Tessa I may be a little late for dinner."

Duncan patted Micah's back. "Thanks, man."

"No problem. Congratulations. Kyle told me you're going to be his best man."

"Thanks. I'm planning to throw a little something at my place for everyone to get together either late September or early October. I hope you and Tessa can come."

"I think I can speak for Tessa when I say we wouldn't miss it."

Duncan went downstairs, leaving the ADA and the police officer to deal with the piece of garbage in his aunt's house. He saw firsthand how easily he'd been duped. An excellent credit score, impeccable letters of reference and a good work history was a mere facade for a man who was a drug abuser and a purveyor of kiddie porn.

He told Viola they were going to the Sanborns while Micah and Officer Cleary escorted Philip Hughes off the premises. His aunt gave him a look that said she didn't believe him, but didn't press the issue.

They walked the four blocks to where the Sanborns lived and where Tessa had set up her Signature Bridals. Duncan whispered to Tessa why Micah was going to be late, and Viola gave her the box with the cheesecake and several bottles of wine from her prized collection.

Duncan was reunited with Tessa's cousin Faith McMillan and her husband Ethan. They'd come to Ivan's earlier that summer to help celebrate Kyle's thirty-ninth birthday.

Tessa introduced him to her older sister Simone and her brother-in-law Raphael Madison. Duncan remembered Kyle telling him about the bride's beautiful sister, and he had to agree with his friend. Simone Whitfield-Madison was stunning, with deeply tanned tawny skin, curly reddish hair and brilliant hazel eyes. There was no doubt she and her blond-haired, blue-eyed husband would have beautiful, exotic-looking children. The doorbell rang and more Whitfields, ranging from seniors to preteens crowded the sofas, loveseats and chairs in the many rooms of the stately brownstone.

Duncan found himself cloistered in a room with the men, discussing everything from President Barack Obama to the Yankees. A good-natured argument erupted when Ethan brought up the topic of the pennant race. Only a few percentage points separated the top two teams in each league and division. Although he'd come with his aunt, Duncan felt the lack of female companionship. The elder Whitfield men had their wives, the Whitfield women their husbands.

He wanted Tamara—he wanted to see her, talk to her, touch her and kiss her. Mixed feelings surged through Duncan as he tried to understand why he was so attracted to Dr. Tamara Wolcott. They'd spent six hours together, but it hadn't been enough for him.

Duncan wanted more—a lot more.

Tamara didn't get out of bed until after noon on Sunday. She showered and pulled on a pair of sweatpants, socks and an oversize T-shirt. Two cups of coffee, a banana and one slice of buttered toast served as brunch. She made her bed, and then crawled back into it to read the stack of magazines that had piled up for months, while music from the radio on the bedside table played softly. She'd just finished reading an article in *W* when the phone rang.

Reaching over, she picked up the cordless phone, mumbling a greeting.

"Tamara, is that you?"

She put down the magazine. "Who else would it be, Renata?"

"It didn't sound like you."

"I can assure you that it is me."

If her sister was calling her it had to be because she wanted money. Her shopaholic sister regularly exceeded her monthly budget whenever she just had to have a new pair of shoes or that cute little outfit. Tamara constantly reminded her that, as an elementary school teacher, the effect of designer shoes and suits would be lost on her young students. But Renata had always been and would always be a fashionista.

"I'm calling because Tiffany and I want to host a surprise sixtieth birthday celebration for Daddy."

"Where are you going to host it?" Tamara asked.

"I'm willing to have it at my house, but Tiff hinted that she wanted it at her place because she just added a party room."

Tamara knew her sisters were notorious for attempting to upstage each other. "Host it in a private room at a restaurant."

"Where, Tamara?"

"That's for you and Tiffany to decide. Either you can have it on Long Island or the city."

"If you can check out some restaurants in Manhattan I'll check them out here."

"How many people do you expect to invite?"

"Sixty. That's going to be the magic number."

Tamara smiled. "I like that. What budget are we working with?"

"Tiff and I figured it would cost about a hundred per person. Add an additional thousand for an open bar."

"What if we throw in three thousand each? That should cover everything, including tax and gratuity. Do you want to have it on that day or on the weekend? Try to keep in mind that weekends are more expensive." This year their father's birthday fell on a Thursday.

"I prefer celebrating on his actual birthday."

"What about the menu?" Tamara asked.

"That would depend on the restaurant."

Tamara thought of a midtown restaurant overlooking the Hudson River and made a mental note to call the Hudson Terrace. "Are you going to have a problem coming up with your share of the costs?" she asked Renata.

"I'll borrow the money from my credit union."

"What's up with you, Renata?" Tamara asked in a quiet voice.

"What are you talking about?" Renata's tone had hardened, taking on an edge.

"Are you and Lenny having financial problems?" The sound of weeping came through the earpiece, shocking Tamara. Although her sister always called to ask to borrow money, Renata always repaid her. "Renata, talk to me."

"I...I can't. I have to hang up."

Tamara held the receiver until a shrill beeping sound forced her to return the handset to its base. Instinctively, she knew Renata was hiding some-thing—*but what?* she mused. She would wait until tomorrow, after her brother-in-law left the house to go to work, then call Renata.

Sinking against the mound of pillows supporting her back, Tamara closed her eyes. She'd never been one to get involved in her sisters' personal lives, because they seemed to live charmed existences. They had the perfect husbands, homes and children. Both had purchased McMansions in the affluent Wheatley Heights community. Vaulted ceilings, marble floors, massive chandeliers and floor-to-ceiling windows greeted visitors when Renata or Tiffany opened the doors to their homes.

Whenever her sisters ventured into the city they refused to come to Tamara's apartment because they didn't want to walk up five flights of stairs. Not so her parents, who loved Manhattan and preferred staying with their daughter than in a midtown hotel.

Tamara always adjusted her schedule to spend time with them. Either she took them out for brunch or prepared their favorite breakfast foods.

She jumped, startled when someone rang the downstairs bell. Swinging her legs over the side of the bed, Tamara went to the door and pressed a button on the intercom. "Who is it?"

"Trenz Florist. I have a delivery for a Tamara Wolcott."

She pushed the button to disengage the lock on the downstairs door, wondering who could've sent her flowers. Opening the closet in the foyer, Tamara reached for a small wooden box on the top shelf. In it were a stack of singles, her tip stash for dry cleaning, laundry and groceries deliveries. Carrying bags up five flights of stairs was not something she relished.

Tamara opened the door when she heard the soft tap. A young man handed her a large bouquet of bloodred and hot-pink roses in a glass vase. She signed the receipt, handing him a tip, and he thanked her profusely. Plucking the card off the cellophane, she read the neat printing: Thank you for a wonderful evening; we must do it again! Duncan."

"And we *will* do it again," she whispered aloud.

She removed the cellophane and carried the vase into the living room, where she set it down on a table amongst a collection of Waterford crystal votives. The sweet scent of the flowers wafted into her nostrils.

Returning to the bedroom, she picked up her cell phone and dialed the number to Duncan's cell. A smile softened her mouth when she heard his soothing baritone. "I want to thank you."

"Thank me for what, Tamara?"

"For sending me flowers."

"I hope you like them."

"I love them. They're beautiful."

"So are you."

"Easy, Duncan, or you'll give me a swelled head."

"Better your head swelling than mine." A groan came through the earpiece. "I can't believe I just said that."

"Yeah, you did," Tamara teased. "Where are you, Duncan?"

"I'm in Brooklyn visiting my aunt. Why?"

"I thought maybe I'd treat you to dinner."

"I just ate. What about you?"

"I haven't eaten yet."

"I could stop by and take you out so you can eat." Tamara shook her head although Duncan couldn't see her. "Don't bother. I'll either fix something light or order in."

"I'll take you out."

"But you've already eaten, Duncan."

"I'll have coffee, or I'll watch you eat. I'll be leaving here in about half an hour. Look for me sometime around six."

Tamara smiled. "Okay. I'll be ready at six."

"I'm wearing jeans, so it'll have to be a casual place to eat."

"That's not a problem."

"I'll see you at six."

Tamara ended the call, then did a happy dance, twirling around the room. Duncan sending her flowers had given her an excuse to call him. What she was forced to acknowledge was that she'd wanted to see him again.

What she refused to acknowledge was that she wanted to sleep with Duncan Gilmore.

Chapter 7

Tamara answered the intercom, pushing the button to unlock the downstairs door when Duncan announced himself. She was standing with the door open when he stepped off the landing carrying two bulging plastic bags.

Water dripped off the bill of his cap.

When he raised his head she noticed he was wearing glasses. The spectacles did little to distract from his overall attractiveness. In fact, they made him appear handsomely bookish. "It's pouring, so I decided to stop and bring in dinner," he explained, setting the wet bags on the straw mat outside the door.

"Give me your cap and jacket," she ordered. "I'll hang them up in the bathroom."

Duncan took them off, shaking out the moisture. "Should I take off my shoes?"

"You can leave them on the mat under the table in the foyer. I didn't realize it was raining that hard."

"It just started pouring." He handed Tamara his clothes, then kicked off his running shoes and placed them on the mat.

Duncan liked rain, but only when he was inside looking out. The days it rained and he didn't have to go into the office he usually sat on his terrace staring through the raindrops. Those were times when he read, ate and slept there if there was little or no wind.

His gaze lingered on Tamara as she turned and walked into the apartment with his wet clothes. She looked nothing like the woman from the night before who had been dressed to the nines. Today she wore a pair of loose-fitting sweats and an oversized T-shirt. The baggy attire successfully camouflaged her curvy body. Picking up the bags, he entered the apartment, closing and locking the door behind him.

Last night he hadn't gone any farther than the front door, but today he saw the space Tamara called home. Her apartment was small, but exquisitely furnished. Silk throw pillows in a vibrant aubergine completed two facing loveseats in supple dove-gray leather. The color scheme was repeated in the pale-gray walls and the purple-patterned area rug with gray and white accents. Mahogany side tables topped with lead-crystal-based lamps with silk pleated shades matched a table positioned along a wall which bore a collection of crystal votives. The bouquet of roses was a bright splash of color against the wall. The lamps were turned to the lowest setting making the room look soft and romantic.

He walked into the kitchen, only steps ahead of Tamara. The room functioned as both kitchen and dining room. The work area was designed in a small triangle for optimal ease and efficiency. A dining bar was built into one side of the center island, offering a spot to sit, snack or relax while meals were prepared.

An antique cupboard in an alcove that was set up as a dining area was filled with china. A rustic table with two long cushioned benches positioned along its length replaced the usual dining set. Mismatched armchairs with quilted cushioned seats faced each other at either end of the table. The design of the pewter hanging-light fixture was in keeping with the dining area's personality.

"Very nice," he said, meeting Tamara's expectant gaze. "I like your place." The kitchen work area was ultramodern with the stainless-steel sink and appliances, while the dining area made him feel as if he'd stepped back in time.

"Thank you." She pointed to his jeans. "If you

want to get out of those pants, I can give you a pair of sweats or scrubs."

"Your clothes won't fit me."

"But my roommate's will."

Duncan placed the bags on the butcher-block island to keep from dropping them. "You have a roommate?"

"Just temporarily."

"Is your roommate a guy?"

"Yes, Duncan, he's a guy."

He clenched his teeth so tightly a muscle jumped noticeably in his jaw. "Is he here now?"

Tamara opened the bags and took out several Chinese-style takeout containers. "No. He's spending the weekend out east. He's not going to be back until tomorrow. Rodney's shifts rotate. He's usually on days for two weeks, then nights for two weeks."

The revelations that Tamara had a roommate— albeit temporary—and that the roommate was a man made Duncan feel as if he'd been blindsided. He wondered if the man he'd seen her with at the diner was the roommate, a man she'd said was her colleague.

"Is he the one I saw you with at the diner?" Duncan knew he sounded like a jealous lover, but he didn't care. Although it was unattractive, his pos-sessiveness had surfaced.

"Yes." Tamara didn't offer any more information as she continued emptying the bags.

"How long will he live with you?"

Something in Duncan's voice garnered her rapt attention, and she stopped what she'd been doing to stare at him. "Don't tell me you're jealous?"

There was no way Duncan was going to admit that he was jealous. To do so would make him appear weak, vulnerable—something he didn't want to be. "No."

Tamara winked at him. "Good. I don't want my friendship with Rodney to jeopardize our friendship."

"Do you kiss all of your male friends the way you kissed me last night?"

"No. Rodney is a friend and colleague, and unfortunately I had to learn the hard way never to combine business and pleasure."

Duncan realized Tamara had just served notice she would never become his client or he her patient, a situation that would prove conducive and advantageous for them to take their *friendship* to another level.

"I'll take either the scrubs or sweats." The rain-soaked jeans felt clammy against his skin.

"I'll be right back. Meanwhile, take off your jeans and hang them over the shower rod."

He gave her an incredulous stare. "You expect me to strip down here?"

Tamara rolled her eyes at him. "There is nothing you have I haven't seen every day since becoming a doctor."

"The difference is you haven't seen *mine*."

"Don't tell me you're reluctant to take off your pants because you go commando."

"What do you know about going commando?"

"A lot of men come into the E.R. sans underwear. Most of them say they find underwear restricting."

"Anything is restricting if it's too small."

Throwing back her head, Tamara laughed heartily. "Please, let's not talk about people wearing too-small garments. I had a patient come into the E.R. with a certain part of his anatomy swollen to twice its size because he liked wearing his wife's thong panties. He confessed that she'd come home unexpectedly so he'd pulled up his pants, still wearing the thong. It was another four hours before he was able to take them off, but by that time he was in agony. When I first asked him how he'd sustained his injury he lied, saying he was playing baseball and someone had accidentally hit him in the groin. But when I saw the deep imprint of where the elastic had bitten into his flesh he confessed. He pleaded with me not to tell his wife that he liked dressing up in her underwear. I reassured him I was bound by doctor-patient confidentiality."

Duncan struggled not to laugh. "Were he and his wife about the same size?"

Tamara chuckled. "No. She weighed about one-twenty and he was twice that much."

Duncan affected a grimace. "Ouch."

"You've got that right. I gave him some medication to take the edge off the pain and told him to apply cold compresses to bring down the swelling."

"Did you tell him to stay away from his wife's lingerie drawer?"

"Even if I told him that, I knew he wasn't going to take my advice. What I did tell him was to go to a store that sold plus-size garments and buy something closer to his size and weight."

"No, you didn't tell him that!"

"Yes, I did, Duncan. I knew he wasn't going to stop cross-dressing or wearing women's underwear, so I wanted to save the man another embarrassing trip to the E.R. and permanent injury to his gonads."

He shook his head. "You really must see some strange things in the E.R."

"Try bizarre. I'll be right back with your scrubs. I don't need you catching a chill. Then I'd have to treat you."

Duncan brought his hand to his mouth, faking a cough. "I feel a cold coming on." He coughed again. "Does the doctor make house calls?"

Tamara laughed at his antics. "For you, yes."

Turning on her heel, she walked out of the kitchen to Rodney's bedroom. Her roommate favored loose-fitting tunics and drawstring pants, and had purchased dozens to wear when lounging around the apartment. She selected a light-blue set.

Rodney was the ideal roommate. He was quiet and neat. Tamara didn't have to concern herself with picking up after him, and he had heeded her warning not to water her plants. She'd rescued the exotic bonsai plants from the doctors' lounge where they'd been sorely neglected. It had taken more than a year of cutting, grafting, pruning and feeding them to return them to health. The plants, along with her collection of crystal votives, made her apartment feel like home.

Duncan rose to his feet when Tamara walked back into the kitchen. He was thankful that the situation with his aunt's tenant had ended without fanfare. As promised, Internal Affairs Officer Jackson Cleary had called for an unmarked car to take Philip Hughes to the local station house. Police technicians were dispatched to the apartment to seize his computer and search every inch of space for more evidence of the teacher's involvement in child pornography. What Duncan found frightening was that the man had had direct access to children every day of his fifteen-year career.

Duncan had waited until he walked with his aunt home to reveal the perversion of the man who'd lived so close to her. And for the first time in twenty-four years he heard his aunt use profanity, her response shocking him into silence. Once she recovered from her explosive diatribe, she apologized so demurely that Duncan couldn't stop laughing. When he teased her about "going ghetto," Viola was quick to say she had to work and pray every day to maintain a ladylike demeanor.

Duncan took the hospital attire from Tamara and went to the bathroom to change out of his wet clothes. Tamara probably thought he was reticent about undressing in front of her, but nothing was further from the truth. In fact, he was rather comfortable with his body and his views toward sex. He hadn't believed the myths that he would go blind or crazy if he masturbated, that he couldn't get a woman pregnant if he pulled out before ejaculating, or that the beauty of the nude body was only acceptable in art. Stripping off his shirt and jeans, he hung them over the shower rod before he slipped into the scrubs.

Walking on sock-covered feet, he entered the kitchen to find Tamara had turned on an under-the-counter television. The television was tuned to a cable station featuring classic movies. The grotesque image of Charles Laughton as Quasimodo filled the screen.

"'Why can't I be made of stone like these?'" Duncan intoned dramatically.

Tamara froze. She hadn't heard Duncan come back into the kitchen. Her eyes widened in surprise when she stared at him in the scrubs. She was mistaken. He and Rodney weren't similar in size. Duncan's tailored clothes were a foil for a lean, hard body incongruent with someone who spent hours sitting at a desk. She'd bragged about not being affected by a man's naked body, yet she found herself staring numbly at the mat of crisp hair displayed in the V-neck of the tunic.

She blinked slowly, as if coming out of a trance. "You must have seen this film a lot to remember the dialogue."

Duncan closed the distance between them. "I think I lost count after the fifth time. My aunt is a black-and-white-film buff. Whenever a movie house showed a retrospective of films dating back to the 1930s she took me with her. At the time, I would've preferred *Star Wars* and *Indiana Jones*."

"Which of the Laughton films is your favorite?" Tamara asked Duncan.

"It's a tie between *Mutiny on the Bounty* and *Les Misérables*."

"I thought he was truly magnificent as Inspector Javert."

"But he was diabolical as Captain Bligh," Duncan argued good-naturedly. He and Tamara continued their discussion of classic films as she opened containers.

"How on earth do you expect me to eat all this food?" Duncan had bought her Chinese, Caribbean and Indian cuisine.

"I bought enough so you'd have leftovers."

"Thank you, but I'm going to pack up some so that *you* can have leftovers." She held up a hand when he shook his head. "Please don't argue with me, Duncan. This is entirely too much food, even for two people." All totaled, he'd bought eight containers, each with a different selection.

Duncan flashed a sheepish grin. "I have a confession to make."

"What is it?"

"I don't cook."

Tamara stared at Duncan, baffled. "You don't know how to heat up leftovers?"

"I don't heat up leftovers because I only order enough food for a single meal."

Resting her elbows on the butcher-block counter, she leaned closer to him. "You *don't* cook or you *can't* cook?"

Duncan, assuming a similar pose, leaned forward until their noses were inches apart. "I don't."

Tamara met his eyes behind the lenses of his glasses. "Why not?"

"I don't know how to cook for one person."

"All you have to do is follow a recipe that serves two, then half everything."

"That's too complicated. My life is about simplicity."

"Do you want me to show you how it's done?"

"Will you?" he asked.

"I will, but only if you want, Duncan."

"I want…" he whispered, his words trailing off. Rising slightly he angled his head as he pressed his lips to hers, caressing her mouth until her lips parted.

Tamara swallowed a groan as Duncan's mouth began a gentle sensual assault on hers. One moment she was leaning and the next she'd straightened as Duncan pulled her to his chest. He fastened his mouth along the column of her neck, pressing a kiss there.

Bracing his hips against the edge of the island, Duncan eased Tamara to stand between his outspread legs. He smiled, and she returned it. Her hair, a mass of tiny curls, framed her face and the nape of her neck in sensual disarray. He wanted to tell her what he was feeling but didn't want to move too quickly. They hadn't known each other a week, yet Duncan felt as if he'd known Tamara Wolcott forever.

Tamara's eyelids fluttered wildly when she felt the hardness of Duncan's thighs brushing against hers. She saw desire in his gaze and knew she felt the same. She felt the gentle strength of his fingers on her upper arms and wanted to get closer, yet she was afraid to move because if she did it would communicate wordlessly how much she wanted and needed this stranger to make love to her.

"Duncan—"

"Don't say anything," he whispered, interrupting her. "Please, let's enjoy this moment."

Smiling, Tamara closed her eyes and rested her head against his shoulder. She inhaled what now had become the familiar scent of his aftershave. Her arms went around his neck. She didn't know how, but Tamara could feel Duncan's heartbeat in her ears keeping time with her own.

She lost track of how long they stood together in a comforting, healing embrace. However, when she lowered her arms and eased out of his embrace, what she felt was akin to the peace she experienced after climaxing.

"You started to tell me what you want," she said, stepping back to put some space between them.

"I want you to show me how to cook for one person."

"It's easy, Duncan."

"It's easy because you know how to do it. Whenever I prepare a meal I usually make too much, then after a couple of days I throw it out. It's criminal and immoral to throw away food when so many people go hungry not only in this country, but all over the world."

"We'll treat it like a field lesson. It'll be up to you to make up a menu of what you want to eat. We'll go to the market to buy the ingredients, then we'll cook together. It shouldn't take more than three lessons for you to get the hang of it."

"What if I'm a slow learner?"

"You'd better learn fast, because my sister and I have to plan a surprise birthday party for our father and we only have a month to pull it off."

"Where's it going to be held?"

"My sisters are volunteering their homes, but I

believe a restaurant would be a better venue because they won't have to concern themselves with the clean-up."

Duncan told Tamara that he wanted to host a get-together for his friend and his friend's fiancée. "I'm thinking about having it in my home only because the setting would be more intimate than a restaurant or catering hall."

"How many do you intend to invite?"

"I haven't taken a head count."

"Can you give me an approximate head count?" Tamara asked.

Duncan angled his head. "Maybe twenty-five or thirty."

"Sit-down or buffet?"

"I don't know."

"Have you set a date?"

"Yes. It's the third Saturday in September."

Tamara gave him a facetious grin. "Thank goodness for that," she said under her breath.

"I heard that, Dr. Wolcott."

"I meant for you to hear it, Mr. Gilmore. Have you thought of hiring a party planner?"

He gave her a blank stare. "Why hadn't I thought of that?"

"I don't know, Duncan."

He took several steps, leaned over and kissed her cheek. "Thanks for the suggestion. Are you going to hire a planner?"

"Not if we hold it at a restaurant. I'll tell the banquet manager what we want and they'll take care of everything."

Tamara sat down at the dining bar in the island to enjoy a dinner of tandoori chicken, yellow rice and steamed broccoli in a garlic sauce. She finished eating at the same time the credits rolled across the screen, indicating the end of the movie.

Duncan pumped his fist. "*Mutiny* is coming on next."

"If you want, you can watch it in my bedroom." Tamara had given up watching television in the den when Rodney moved in.

"Only if you'll watch it with me," Duncan countered.

She glanced at the clock on the microwave. The movie was scheduled to start in ten minutes. "Go into the bedroom and turn on the TV while I clean up here."

"It'll go faster if I help you."

Tamara was able to store the containers in the refrigerator and rinse and stack her dishes in the dishwasher with Duncan's assistance in half the time that she would have taken alone. Taking his hand, she led him to her bedroom, flopped down on the bed and, using the remote control, turned on the television.

Patting the mattress, she smiled at Duncan. "Come, Duncan, get into bed."

Duncan hesitated. Tamara had invited him to share her bed and he wondered if she would ever invite him to share her body. He got on the bed and propped a mound of pillows against the linen-slip-covered headboard to cradle his back. Pillows, sheets and blankets in monochromatic colors, shades ranging through chocolate brown, café au lait and ecru, complemented the headboard's pale palette. An oatmeal-beige chenille throw was folded at the foot of the bed.

Small round pedestal tables doubled as night-stands, and a cream-colored area rug on the bleached-pine floor gave an open invitation to stay a while. Linen-look woven window treatments provided privacy.

Tamara shifted into a more comfortable position, her shoulder touching Duncan's "Do you want me to adjust the air-conditioning?" She smiled at him.

"Are you cold?"

"A little."

Dropping an arm over Tamara's shoulders, Duncan pulled her to his body. "Let me warm you up."

She snuggled against him, feeling the heat from his body seep into hers. "Nice."

It was the last word Tamara uttered. Halfway through the movie her eyelids fluttered then closed and she fell asleep in Duncan's embrace, as if it was something she'd done often.

She never knew when he flicked off the television and slipped out of bed to change into his clothes. Tamara didn't stir when he opened and closed the self-locking door behind him.

The sun was high in the sky when she woke, fully dressed, to find the space beside her empty, but the scent of aftershave lingering on a pillow. She'd gotten her wish; she'd shared a bed with Duncan Gilmore.

Chapter 8

Tamara met Rodney as he was exiting a train in Pennsylvania Station and she was waiting to board. He looked different. The sun had darkened his face and a reddish stubble had replaced the flyaway curls. He caught her hand, pulling her away from the other riders filing out of Long Island Railroad trains and shuffling toward the staircase.

"What's up, Wolcott?"

She took a breath. "I'm on my way to my sister's place. She called to say she has a dilemma."

Rodney stared at her quilted overnight bag. "How long will you be away?"

"I plan to spend the night. I can only take either of my sisters in very small doses."

Leaning over he kissed her cheek. "Good luck."

"Thank you, Fox."

Tamara boarded the train and sat down in a window seat. She'd told Rodney she expected to spend the night, praying that was all she would stay. It wasn't often that she stayed over with either Renata or Tiffany and if she did it was to placate her nieces and nephews.

Renata wasn't usually prone to tears or histrionics, but when Tamara had answered the phone earlier that morning it was to hysterical crying. She had tried to get Renata to calm down enough to tell her why she was upset, but to no avail. She told Renata to hang up, because she was coming to see her.

Tamara didn't want to believe she was on a train heading for Long Island to comfort a sister who'd made her childhood a living hell. If she hadn't known for certain that Tiffany and Renata were her sisters, Tamara would have felt like Cinderella. Very few days had passed when Renata and Tiff, as Tiffany liked to be called, hadn't teased her about her weight. The teasing had become so mean-spirited that Tamara had stopped eating for long periods of time. The result was intense headaches and fainting spells. She'd lost weight, but at the expense of her health.

One day when watching a TV talk show, Tamara had heard a guest speaker talk about turning a negative into a positive. A person should work to enhance their best qualities rather than focusing on their worst. For Tamara it was her intellect. She had entered pre-kindergarten with a third-grade reading level. She'd accelerated a grade, going from seventh to ninth and had graduated high school with two years of college credits.

It had taken a while, but Tamara had finally realized boys liked pretty *and* brainy girls. That had become more than apparent when she entered college. She had her first very serious relationship, but it had ended when her lover returned to California to start a career in film.

After the conductor punched her ticket, Tamara closed her eyes rather than stare at the landscape whizzing past the fast-moving train. Why, she thought, did Renata have to have a meltdown just when she was starting her vacation? Just when she'd begun dating again?

A secret smile softened Tamara's mouth as she recalled crawling into bed with Duncan to watch television. Being in his arms, sharing his body heat, felt as natural as breathing.

Call it fate, fortune or destiny, but there had to be a reason why she'd been in that high-rise elevator with Duncan Gilmore when it had stopped between floors. She'd thought about it, concluding she didn't want or need an answer. There were some things in life that just happened.

Tamara planned to enjoy her time with Duncan,

and if or when it ended she would be left with memories that would exceed what she'd had with Edward, because this time she had no expectations. She didn't want to marry, she wasn't ready to become a mother and she had a rewarding career. And if things worked out well between her and Duncan, then she could possibly have a rewarding love life.

Tamara stared at her sister, stunned by her weight loss. She doubted whether Renata weighed a hundred pounds. Renata Wolcott-Powell's teenage daughter wore a larger dress size than her mother.

Pulling her gaze away from Renata, who sat zombie-like, her hands cradling a tumbler of vodka as if it were a priceless relic, Tamara glanced around the room where her sister either received visitors or hosted intimate get-togethers. Every piece of furniture and objet d'art was strategically positioned for optimum viewing. The room always reminded Tamara of an art gallery.

"Drinking that isn't going to solve your problem, Renata."

Renata glared at Tamara. "It helps me to forget."

"Forget what?"

Setting down the crystal tumbler on a matching coaster, Renata dabbed her eyes with a crumpled tissue. "I can't talk about it."

Tamara successfully reined in her temper. "I didn't

disrupt my vacation and get on the train to come here for you to tell me that you can't talk about it."

Renata peered at Tamara through puffy eyes. She was drowning in her own self-pity. Tamara had always been prettier and smarter than she and Tiffany, but they'd double-teamed against their youngest sister in an attempt to break her spirit. It had worked for a while, until Tamara brought home her report card. Renata and Tiffany were relegated to the background and Tamara became the center of attention. The praise and compliments usually lasted a week, then she and Tiff resumed their childish reign of terror.

"I thought I could talk about it, Tami, but I'm too ashamed."

Tamara wanted to hear what had upset Renata. She'd come to offer emotional support to a sister who'd methodically and systematically done all she could to humiliate her every chance she got, a sister who'd goaded their middle sister into becoming her willing accomplice. Moselle Wolcott wasn't without blame because whenever Renata or Tiffany overheard their mother mention Tamara's weight it added another tool to their taunting arsenal.

Tamara clenched her teeth in frustration. "I plan to sit here for an hour and then I'm going to call for a taxi to take me back to the station. I'm going to ask you again. How much money do you need?"

Reaching for the tumbler, Renata took a sip of

the clear liquid, grimacing as it slid down the back of her throat and warmed her chest; she knew her youngest sister hadn't issued an idle threat.

"It's no longer about money, Tami."

"Then what is it about?" There was a pregnant pause as the sisters stared at each other. "You call me at least once a month asking for money, then a week or two later you repay me. What's up with that, Renata?"

"I needed the money to pay a private investigator."

Tamara sat up straighter. "What are you talking about?"

"I asked for the money to pay someone to follow Robert."

"Why on earth would you want someone to follow your husband?"

Renata took another sip. "I had to know for certain if my husband was having an *affair!* I cashed the checks you sent me and gave the P.I. cash. I waited until I got paid, then sent you a check. I suppose I could've paid him out of my household account, but I realized that after the fact."

"You're talking in circles, Renata. What made you suspect Robert was or is having an affair?"

"It's no longer a suspicion, Tami. I now have proof that he's sleeping with another woman."

Tamara didn't want to believe that her soft-spoken, nerdy brother-in-law was sleeping around. Duncan thought of himself as a nerd, but he was a sexy nerd. Robert Powell put the *N* in nerd. The forty-year-old pharmaceutical executive had always reminded her of a boy wearing his father's clothes.

"Where's the proof, Renata?"

"You're sitting on it."

It took several seconds for Tamara to stand and lift up the silk-covered chair cushion to find an envelope. She didn't want the photos to be real, but when she glanced at the black-and-white photographs of her brother-in-law and a woman in bed together Tamara felt as if someone had punched her in her face.

She slipped the half dozen photos back into the envelope, handing it to Renata. "What are you going to do?"

"I'm going to divorce him."

Tamara sat down next to Renata, easing the glass from her hand. Her sister's fingers were ice-cold. "Does he know that you know?" Renata shook her head. "Where is he?"

"He's at a conference in Vegas."

Renata's husband was probably in Vegas with his mistress, while their teenage daughters were vacationing in Europe with their maternal grandparents. "When is he expected back?"

"Thursday."

"Are you going to divorce him without hearing his side?"

"Side, Tamara? There is no side. The pictures tell the whole story. My husband is screwing another woman. I knew something was wrong when he wouldn't touch me. A woman shouldn't have to beg her husband to make love to her. At first I thought it was because we've been married so long that we'd lost the spark. But from those photos you can see that Robert doesn't have a problem lighting up that *ho*."

Here we go, Tamara mused. Renata was already primed to go into her name-calling repertoire. She felt her sister's pain because she knew firsthand about a duplicitous husband. He'd left her financially destitute, homeless and without her only companion.

"Have you contacted a lawyer?" she asked Renata.

"Not yet."

"That's the first thing you need to do, so you know what your options are."

"I only have one option—get rid of the bastard."

"You also need to protect yourself and your children, Renata. You have to get a lawyer who will look after your interests or you'll end up like me."

Renata sniffled. "I suppose I can call Barry."

"Who's Barry?"

"He's a friend."

Tamara lifted her eyebrows. "Whose friend?"

"He's a friend of the family."

"That's your first mistake, Renata. You cannot get someone who knows you and Robert to represent you. Can't you think of anyone else?"

Renata pressed the back of her hand to her forehead. "I can't think right now."

"That's because you're drunk and starved. I want you to go take a shower and change your clothes."

"Why?"

Rising to her feet, Tamara pulled Renata gently up from the loveseat. "I'm taking you out so you can get something to eat." There were three eggs, a stick of butter and a container of yogurt in Renata's refrigerator. "And if you don't put on some weight, you won't have to worry about a divorce, because instead of being a divorced man your husband will become a widower. And that means he'll probably move his *ho* into your home to play stepmother to your children. Is that what you want, Renata?"

"I'd kill him."

"No, you wouldn't. You'd be dead. Now go and clean yourself up."

Renata sniffled again. "Can you hang out with me for a couple of days? I really don't want to be alone."

"I will, but you have to promise me something."

"What, Tami?"

"I want you to begin eating. I'm not talking to you as your sister, but as a doctor. I'm certain that if I had to order a complete blood workup on you the results would be frightening. And if you're serious about divorcing Robert, and if you decide you want to start dating again then you'd better take a good look in the mirror. What you'll see staring back at you isn't cute, Renata."

"How much weight do you want me to gain?"

"Enough so that your clavicle isn't so prominent. Right now you have an old woman's neck."

Renata placed a hand over her throat. "But I'm only thirty-eight."

"I know how old you are, Renata. Right now you don't look thirty-eight."

"Are you...you saying I look older?"

Tamara managed a tight smile. "What you look is a hot mess."

"That's not right, Tamara."

"Yeah, I know," Tamara said glibly. "I'm going to call *Je Vous Aime* and make appointments for a day of beauty. I know someone who may be able to help with your legal problems. I'll call and ask him for the name of an attorney."

Tears began welling up in Renata's eyes and then they overflowed. "Why are you helping me when I've been so mean to you, Tami?"

Tamara waved a hand. "Please, Renata. You give yourself too much credit. You and Tiffany were nothing more than annoyances." Most times she'd ignored her sisters, but it was their mother's critical attitude that had been much more emotionally damaging because Tamara had always wanted her mother's approval.

Renata touched her fingertips to her moist cheeks. "Where are we going to eat?"

"What do you feel like eating?"

"Fish."

Tamara searched her memory for a good Long Island seafood restaurant. "I know an excellent one, but it's in Nassau County."

"Hello, city girl. I do have a car," Renata teased. She sobered quickly. "You're going to have to drive because right now I'm under the influence."

"Don't worry, Renata. I'll drive."

"Mr. Gilmore, Mrs. Hamilton has arrived."

Duncan pressed the intercom button on his telephone console. "Give me five minutes and then bring her in, Mia." Pushing back from the desk, Duncan stood and reached for his suit jacket, slipping his arms into the sleeves.

A restlessness had assailed him when he least expected it. It had been four days since he'd seen or heard from Tamara. He'd left her sleeping Sunday night, now he chided himself for not waking her up to let her know he was leaving. He waited until mid-afternoon Monday to call her apartment. He'd left a message on her voice mail for her to return the call. Monday had passed, then Tuesday, Wednesday and Thursday. It was now Friday and she still hadn't called. He'd imagined dozens of scenarios: she'd cut her vacation short and returned to the hospital, she'd fallen ill or she'd decided she didn't want to see him again.

This was the one and only time he'd prayed for more clients so he could lose track of time as he put in twelve-hour days, shutting out everything around him. It wasn't his busiest time of year, but days before the official end of the summer season. Kyle and his fiancée Ava were hosting a small gathering at their Strivers' Row townhouse for friends and family on the Labor Day weekend. Ava had promised to give him the names and addresses of the guests for the soirée he was planning in their honor.

It had been more than a decade since he'd seen Gail Hamilton. The incredibly wealthy widow had been his client when he'd worked for CEMS Investments. When he'd handed in his resignation after he'd made the decision to set up his own accounting and financial planning venture, he hadn't contacted any of his former clients. Several of them managed to find him, but Duncan refused to take them on because they were used to aggressive trading and he'd become less of a risk-taker.

He affected a warm smile for the platinum-haired, fifty-something widow when Mia escorted her into his office. It was as if time had stood still. The elegantly dressed woman looked exactly the same as she had a decade before.

Gail Hamilton offered Duncan Gilmore a manicured hand, her violet eyes shimmering like polished tanzanite. A recent Botox treatment prevented her from smiling. "Duncan. How long has it been?"

A two-pack-a-day cigarette habit had thickened her vocal cords and deepened her voice to a throaty growl. Smoking had not only affected her throat, but had also ravaged her skin until she'd undergone hypnosis to rid herself of the habit. She'd paid her plastic surgeon a small fortune to take fifteen years off her face. What she hadn't been able to correct were the nicotine stains on her fingers. A quack dermatologist had attempted dermabrasion, laser removal and eventually a bleaching technique, but he hadn't been able to erase them completely. Her hands weren't perfect, but she now felt comfortable enough go out without wearing gloves.

Duncan shook her hand, his expressive eyebrows lifting when he stared intently at her face. "Ten years."

"Ten years, six months and eleven days. It's taken me that long to track you down."

"I didn't realize I was that difficult to find," he replied with a facetious smile. "Please come and sit down." He directed her to an alcove in the spacious office, seating her in a straight-backed dark-brown-leather chair. He sat down opposite her.

Duncan had thought it was his imagination ten years before, but he was even more certain now that Gail Hamilton wasn't as interested in Duncan Gilmore monitoring her investments as she was in Duncan Gilmore.

By the time he entered high school, he'd exchanged his glasses for contact lenses and replaced his adolescent awkwardness with a fluid grace that garnered the attention of the opposite sex. And

"What happens to Bank of America or Alcoa does not concern me, Duncan."

He struggled not to lose his temper. "What affects Alcoa, banks and Fortune 500 companies affects all of us, Mrs. Hamilton. The grim realty of 2008 only confirmed what investors had known for months. It was a very bad year to own stocks. And I mean any stocks. Almost no industry was spared."

Gail leaned forward, giving Duncan a better view of the enhanced cleavage under her suit jacket. "What I don't want is to lose more money."

"If you've come to me because you believe I have the magic potion to help you recoup what you've lost, then you're mistaken." His tone had lost its normally velvet quality. "The only thing I can do for you is to advise you where you can invest what's left in something that I know is ultra-safe."

"Where is that?"

"United States Treasury securities."

Gail sat back. "You want me to invest in the government? Aren't they the ones who let this subprime mortgage mess get out of control?"

"I'm certain you didn't come to me for a lesson in economics, Mrs. Hamilton. The only thing I'm going to say on the matter is that no industry was spared as the subprime mortgage market metastasized like a cancer and sank our economy into what could be a long recession. Right now I'm advising my clients to buy U.S. Treasury securities. Many investors, having lost stocks and other investments, are buying them. The advantage to this is that they're safe, and the only disadvantage is they offer little or no return. Most who invest are simply content to get their money back, not lose it."

"My broker at CEMS told me he was going for diversification because he felt it unwise for me to put all of my eggs in one basket. Well, diversification got me jack, because he put a lot of my money into so-called BRIC economies, or whatever the hell that is."

Duncan nodded. "BRIC is an acronym for Brazil, Russia, India and China. They were targeted countries for brokers when the market was booming because they have what economists deem emerging economies. The stock crisis is not only in this country but worldwide. Stocks in developed European and Asian markets also fell sharply, but less than their emerging counterparts. Many commodities like copper and oil crashed."

Gail's eyes narrowed. "You're right, Duncan. I didn't come here for an economics lesson, but apparently I'm going to hear one."

"I usually give all my clients a mini-lesson. Investing in the market is like going to a casino. You only invest what you can afford to lose."

"I lost more than I wanted to lose."

"Did you ask your broker to give you a printout of your account activity?" Duncan asked.

When he'd worked for CEMS he'd made it a practice to give his clients a monthly statement. When the CEO discovered what he'd been doing he was given a verbal dressing-down. But when Duncan reminded the arrogant executive that there was no written company rule that he couldn't send out a monthly statement to his clients, a memorandum was circulated before the end of the day that only accounting was authorized to mail out statements. A written request from a client for a statement other than the bi-annual ones needed the CEO's signature.

"I got the ones for the period ending June thirtieth, December thirty-first and the first six months of this year."

Lowering his leg, feet planted apart on the area rug, Duncan gave her a long, penetrating stare. "I want you to submit a written request for a printout of your monthly activity for the past eighteen months. Address the letter, certified return receipt, directly to the CEO. Make certain you indicate a deadline date as to when you expect to have the statements. I also want you to request an audit. Not an internal audit, but one done by an outside firm. Once you get them, call my executive assistant to set up another appointment."

"What would you look for, Duncan?"

"I'm not certain."

It was a half truth. He suspected CEMS executives were concealing risky transactions, thereby misleading their clients. The statements may have posted losses when there may have been gains. And if Duncan discovered an irregularity, then he would refer Gail Hamilton to Chatham and Wainwright. Kyle Chatham and his partner Jordan Wainwright were well-versed in securities fraud; they'd worked together at a prestigious New York law firm handling cases ranging from corporate espionage to capital murder. He stood up, indicating the meeting had concluded, and extended his hand to assist the flirtatious widow.

"Would you mind joining me for lunch? My driver is waiting outside."

Duncan angled his head, smiling. "I wish I could, Mrs. Hamilton, but I have another appointment." He released her hand. He was scheduled to meet with another client, but not until later that afternoon.

"When we meet again, I'd like it to be at my pied-à-terre."

Resting a hand in the small of her back, Duncan steered Gail Hamilton toward the door. "We'll talk about it after I go over the statements." He refused to commit to a meeting in one of her two homes. She owned a Fifth Avenue condo and a Long Island mansion overlooking the Sound. Mia Humphrey stood up when he gave her a surreptitious wink. His executive assistant was more than familiar with the gesture.

"Mrs. Hamilton, Ms. Humphrey will escort you out."

Mia's stoic expression didn't change. "Please follow me, Mrs. Hamilton." She'd taken an instant dislike to the woman who appeared to look down her nose at her. And when Mrs. Hamilton called for an appointment she'd insisted on calling her boss *Duncan* rather than *Mr. Gilmore*. Duncan insisted on formality whenever clients were present. The only time she, Augustin and Duncan addressed one another by their given names was when they were out of earshot of clients. Formality fostered professionalism, familiarity a lack of respect.

Duncan walked back into his office, closed the door, slipped off his jacket, loosened his tie and activated the Do not Disturb feature on his phone. He strode over to the alcove and lay across the leather sofa. Closing his eyes, he willed his mind blank and fell asleep. His mind had been in tumult since he'd left the message on Tamara's voice mail and she hadn't gotten back to him.

A fear that something had happened to her reopened a wound and rekindled fears he believed he'd put to rest.

Chapter 9

Duncan swung his legs off the sofa. Reclining had allowed him to relax. He was scheduled to meet with a new client, and initial meetings were usually long, with a litany of ongoing questions. Many of his Harlem clients couldn't afford to take the risks as he'd executed with those who'd signed with CEMS.

Clients like Gail Hamilton were self-centered, greedy and impatient. They expected their brokers to work miracles. Anytime their portfolios were in the seven-figure range their attitudes changed, they became more demanding and at times quite aggressive. They checked the stock prices on the Internet, television cable channels dedicated solely to finance and read the *Wall Street Journal* from the first page to the last.

The longer Duncan had worked at CEMS the more he'd come to respect the clients who tended to micromanage their accounts. Who better to watch one's own money than oneself?

However, the risks he initiated on behalf of the firm's clients did not apply to him when he set up his own portfolio. Duncan invested only what he could afford to lose. He'd begun with an initial investment of twenty-five-thousand dollars, doubled that the second year, and within four years the bottom-line figure in his personal portfolio was staggering. After purchasing the condo, he withdrew all but ten percent, reinvesting in treasury bills and municipal bonds, also known as "munis."

He returned to his desk and buzzed Mia. "Do I have any messages?"

"You have four, Duncan. Micah Sanborn called from the Kings County DA's office. He said you can call him back at your convenience. He left numbers where you can reach him."

Duncan knew Micah was calling him about his aunt's former tenant, who was out on bail, out of the classroom and living with his mother in Queens. "What's the second one?"

"It's from Ava Warrick. She asked for your e-mail addy because she's sending a mailing list you'd asked for."

Clicking a button on the wireless mouse, Duncan saw that Kyle's fiancée had sent him the names and addresses for the get-together at his condo. He downloaded the attachment and printed out two copies. One he would leave in the office and the other he would take home. Ava had sent him a list of twenty-three names. The starred ones indicated those who would bring a guest.

"I got it, Mia. Who else called?"

"A Mrs. Fletcher called to say your order is complete, and you can pick up everything tomorrow morning any time after ten."

A smile of complete satisfaction deepened attractive lines around Duncan's eyes. "Please call the car service and have a driver pick me up at my house tomorrow morning at nine."

Duncan never had to follow up on whatever he told Mia. She'd been referred to him by a social services agency which sought to employ Harlem residents in Harlem-based businesses. When Mia had come in for an interview, her only marketable skill was the ability to answer the telephone in a businesslike manner. Her computer knowledge was limited to the Internet.

When he suggested she take some part-time business courses to improve her skills, courses he'd offered to pay for, Mia had told him she couldn't afford to pay a babysitter to watch her toddler daughter who attended a state-funded daycare center during the day.

Duncan paid for the business courses *and* the cost of babysitting and his investment in Mia Humphrey was repaid tenfold. Her organizational skills proved invaluable during the tax season. "What's the last call?"

"Dr. Wolcott. She wants you to call her because she needs a referral for a divorce attorney."

He whispered a silent prayer of gratitude. She'd gotten back to him. "Did Dr. Wolcott leave a number?"

"Yes. It's her cell."

"Please give it to me."

Duncan wrote down the number and then repeated it. When Tamara had called him, the number that had come up on his ID was her home number. He didn't have her cell number or a number at the hospital. He knew it was probably easier to reach her through the hospital but hadn't wanted to breach the boundaries Tamara had established. If she'd wanted him to have her alternate numbers she would have offered them.

"The receptionists are ordering lunch for the building. Do you want anything?"

"No, thank you. My one o'clock meeting won't be in the office." Duncan had made it a practice not to see first-time clients in the office because he discovered people were more relaxed when conducting business while eating and drinking. "I'm going to return these calls, then I'll be out of the office for the rest of the day."

Duncan decided to call Micah first. He called his office number, but was informed that the ADA was meeting with a judge, and wouldn't be available until later that afternoon. He hung up without leaving a message, knowing he could always reach him at home.

Taking a quick glance at his watch, Duncan noted the time. He had to leave within fifteen minutes to get to the Upper-East-Side restaurant before his potential client arrived. He'd learned early in his business career that he should always arrive at a designated location at least a quarter of an hour before his client. A late arrival indicated not only a lack of respect, but also a total disregard for the other's importance.

He dialed the number of Tamara's cell, his fingers drumming nervously on the top of the desk as he waited for the connection. "Hello, Duncan," she said in singsong.

Duncan smiled. "Hello, Tamara. How are you?"

"I'm good. Did your secretary give you my message?"

"Yes she did. Did you get my message?"

"What message, Duncan?"

"I called you Monday."

"I've been away since Monday, and I hadn't bothered to pick up my messages. What did you say?"

"You'll find out when you listen to the message."

"That's not fair, Duncan."

"What's fair is once you get a boyfriend you should always check your voice mail."

There came a beat. "Is that what you are? A boyfriend?"

"What else can I be, Tamara? I'm definitely not your lover."

Another pause ensued before Tamara said, "I can't respond to that now because I'm in a public place."

"Where are you?"

"I'm in the waiting room of a train station. I'm on my way back to the city."

Duncan sobered. He'd hoped she would respond to his reference to being her boyfriend. "You were asking about a divorce attorney."

"Yes. I know someone who's thinking of divorcing her husband and she would like a consultation before she files the necessary papers."

"I know Kyle doesn't take on divorce cases, but I'll let you talk to him. I'm going to put you on hold while I call him." Duncan hit speed dial for Kyle's private number and listened to a recording that Kyle Chatham would be out of the office and would return the Tuesday following the holiday weekend. He reconnected with Tamara. "He's out of the office until after Labor Day."

The entire building would be closed the following day. He, Ivan and Kyle had agreed when they'd set up their businesses in the brownstone that they would give their employees the day off the Friday before a holiday weekend. They would be given a four-instead of a three-day weekend.

"Damn," she whispered, "I suppose I'm not going to get anyone until after the holiday."

"If you're really anxious to talk to Kyle, then come with me to his place this weekend."

"What's happening this weekend?"

"He and his fiancée are hosting a cookout on Sunday."

"Duncan, I'm certain he's not going to be in a mood to talk business at a cookout."

"He will if I ask him."

"You're kidding, aren't you?"

"No, Tamara, I'm not kidding. Kyle, Ivan and I are as close as brothers. If one of us needs something, then the others step up and do it. No questions asked."

"You guys must have an awesome bond."

"We do," Duncan confirmed without a hint of guile. "Now to change the subject. When am I going to see you again?"

"Are you free tomorrow night?"

He smiled. "It just so happens that I am. In fact I'm free all day tomorrow. What do you want to do?"

"Are you ready for your cooking lessons?"

"Yes. But we don't have to start tomorrow night."

"Yes, we do, Duncan. It's futile to avoid the inevitable."

"We're going to have to go food-shopping."

"Don't worry about that, darling. I'll call in an

order and have it delivered to your place. I plan to give you a crash course in preparing breakfast, lunch and dinner."

Duncan wondered whether Tamara was aware that she'd called him darling. "Are we going to cook at your place?"

"We can't. Remember, I have a roommate."

"Well, since I *don't* have a roommate, then you can stay with me."

"Are you sure you're ready for a house guest?"

"If the guest looks like you, then the answer is yes." Duncan took another glance at his watch. "Look, baby, I'd love to talk some more, but I have a meeting out of the office and I have to leave now or I'll be late."

"Call me at home tonight and we'll set a time to meet tomorrow."

"You've got it. I'll talk to you later."

"La-ter, Dun-can," she sang in singsong.

"La-ter, Ta-ma-ra," he intoned, smiling. He was still smiling when he walked out of the brownstone to hail a taxi to take him to his favorite East-Side restaurant.

Tamara heard the music on the fourth-floor landing, and it became louder and louder as she approached the top floor. There were only two apartments on the fifth floor—hers and that of an elderly couple who'd moved in during the rent-control era. The driving baseline beats of hip-hop, approaching earshattering decibels was coming from her apartment.

Groaning inwardly, Tamara unlocked the door. The volume on her sound system was so high that she was unable to understand the lyrics or identify the hip-hop artist. She had to talk to Rodney about the loud music because the last thing she wanted or needed was problems with her neighbors.

She kicked off her shoes, set her bag on the floor and dropped a stack of mail on the foyer table. Walking on bare feet, she made her way through the living room, coming up short when Rodney walked out of the bathroom without a stitch of clothing on.

Her jaw dropped. "Whoa!"

"Sorry."

She and Rodney had spoken in unison.

Tamara recovered first and turned on her heel, heading for her bedroom. She didn't mind Rodney staying with her, but he couldn't walk around naked, and he couldn't play his music that loud. She hadn't taken more than three steps when the music stopped.

Sitting on the padded bench at the foot of her bed she thought about the three days she'd spent in Wheatley Heights with Renata when she'd wanted to spend that time with Duncan.

Tamara smiled. Even when she spoke to him by phone she felt as if he was right there with her, that a vaguely sensuous sensation came through the phone to wrap her in a cocoon of longing and protection.

She remembered he said he'd left a message on her voice mail. Moving off the bench, she reached for the phone and punched in the code to retrieve her messages. There were three—one from Renata, who thanked her for being there for her. The second was from a clerk at a bookstore who'd called to say the book she wanted had come in. The last one was from Duncan: "Tamara, this is Duncan. Please do not invite me to share your bed again, and then expect me to walk away without making love to you."

She closed her eyes as the impact of his sensual warning seeped into her, bringing with it heat, then chills. When they'd gotten into bed together to watch the movie she hadn't planned on falling asleep. She hadn't known when he'd turned off the television, the bedside lamp or when he had left her apartment.

"Wolcott."

Tamara turned to find Rodney standing outside the bedroom. He'd put on a pair of jeans with a T-shirt. "Yes, Fox?"

"I'm sorry about flashing my naked ass."

She smiled. "Try and remember I'm not your girlfriend. I don't need to see your family jewels. And, you can't play your music that loud. I have elderly neighbors at the end of the hall who—"

"I understand," Rodney interrupted. "It won't happen again. By the way, I have a couple interested in the condo. The bank has preapproved them because they're willing to offer a thirty-percent down payment. I hope I'll be out of your hair by the beginning of October."

Tamara stared at her friend, thinking he seemed more boy than man. He looked even younger with his shorn scalp. "I told you before that you can take all the time you need to find a place."

"That sounds good now, but what's going to happen when you invite a man home? He's not going to be that understanding when you tell him your roommate is a man. I know I wouldn't if you were my woman."

"I'm not your woman, Rodney."

"Whose woman are you, Tamara?"

"Mind your own business, Fox."

"He better be good to you."

"Or what?" she asked.

"You don't want to know."

"Don't tell me you're jealous, Fox."

Rodney shook his head. "I'm not jealous. Just think of me as your overprotective older brother."

She winked at him. "Okay, big brother."

Rodney returned the wink. "I'd better get going."

"Are you working tonight?" Tamara asked.

"Yeah. But this is the last night. On Tuesday I start days."

Tamara stared at the space where Rodney had been. She had to get up and unpack her luggage, sort laundry for a pickup and call in a grocery order for a Chelsea delivery. Duncan had reassured her that she'd be able to talk to his friend about her sister's marital problems, and as much as she hadn't wanted to be drawn into the domestic fray, she had to support Renata. After all, blood was thicker than water.

Duncan, waiting for Tamara to exit the elevator, schooled his expression not to show what he was feeling at that moment. It was as if he'd been waiting an eternity for someone like her to fill up the empty space in his life left by the loss of not one but two women.

Tamara was different from Kalinda Douglas in physical appearance and temperament. He had been drawn to Kalinda because he believed she needed rescuing. Kali affected an air of vulnerability that was palpable, and the first time he'd approached her Duncan knew he would become the one to free her from her cloistered world of strict rules and regulations.

It wasn't until after they'd announced their engagement and he slept with her for the first time that he realized the woman to whom he'd pledged his love and future wasn't what she'd presented. The line in the sand had been drawn when he'd asked her father's permission to marry her, and the official engagement was as binding as an exchange of vows.

The elevator door opened and the woman who'd

occupied his waking thoughts stood before him. He went completely still. Tamara Wolcott was a chameleon. Every time he saw her she looked different. The curly hairdo was missing. She'd straightened her hair, thick strands falling from a natural off-center part to brush her shoulders. A white body-hugging tank top, matching linen walking shorts and black ballet-type shoes exposed and flattered her curvy womanly body.

Reaching for her weekender, Duncan leaned over and brushed a light kiss over her mouth. "Thank you for coming."

Tamara wrapped an arm around Duncan's slender waist. She'd missed him, missed touching and smelling him much more than she wanted to acknowledge—at least openly. "Thank you for inviting me."

Easing back, Duncan stared at her upturned face through the lenses of his glasses. Her fresh-scrubbed face radiated good health. "You don't need an invitation to come over. Anytime you want a change of scene or need a break from your roommate, let me know and I'll make it happen."

Tamara rubbed his back. "I didn't know you were a magic genie. How many wishes do I get?"

Duncan went completely still. Nothing on him moved, not even his eyes, as he held his breath until he was forced to release it. He felt as if he'd stepped back in time. Kali had called him her magical genie because he'd made all of her dreams come true.

He shook his head. "No, Tamara. There's nothing magical about me."

She patted his shoulder, smiling. "If not magical, then you're special."

He forced a smile. "Special?"

Tamara considered Duncan as an unfamiliar rush of total attraction held her spellbound. She'd admitted to him that he was special, but how special? Was he special enough for her to let go of her distrust of men? Special enough for her to open her heart to permit herself to feel love? Special enough to make her think about sharing not only her passion but also her future with a man?

"You're nothing like any other man I've ever known."

"If you're referring to my sleeping with you on Sunday, then I can assure you that it won't happen again."

Tamara met his steady eyes. "I heard your voice-mail message. Let's say I've been warned."

"As long as you understand where I'm coming from, then we should have a good time. Come, let me show you to your bedroom."

Tamara blinked. Duncan was becoming quite adept at segueing from one topic to another without pausing or taking a breath. She followed him across the expansive living/dining room to the staircase. It was apparent she would sleep in the bedroom next to Duncan's.

She'd asked herself over and over whether she wanted to sleep with Duncan, whether she was ready to make love with him, and the answer was a resounding yes. It was after three months of dating that she'd permitted her college boyfriend to share her bed, and she and Edward had met in secret for two years before marrying and sleeping together for the first time the day she celebrated her twenty-second birthday.

Tamara had always been cognizant of her grandmother's warning: act in haste, repent in leisure. With the first two men in her life she'd acted in leisure, but in the end she'd repented in leisure. Edward Bennett had turned her off on *most* men until fate brought her and Duncan Gilmore together.

She'd finally figured out that what had attracted her to Duncan—other than his devastatingly good looks—was his quiet strength. Tamara knew she'd come at him with everything in her verbal arsenal, and he'd parried it with his own comeback that was never insulting or disrespectful.

He cut an elegant figure in tailored suits, custom-made shirts, silk ties and imported footwear, but she preferred the sexy nerd in jeans, T-shirts, running shoes and glasses.

Duncan opened the door to the bedroom, standing aside to let Tamara enter. "Take your time settling in. If there's anything you'll need, just let me know."

She smiled at him. "Thanks. I scheduled a three-o'clock delivery for the groceries. It's almost three, so call me when they come so I can pay the bill."

A slight frown appeared between his eyes. "I'll pay it."

"But it's a lot of—"

Duncan held up a hand, stopping her in mid sentence. "I said I've got it."

Scrunching up her face, Tamara stuck out her tongue at him. She wondered if he'd be so willing to pay the bill when he saw the total. She shopped at one of the most expensive gourmet markets in the city. But it was worth the price because of the quality of the meat, fish, dairy, fruits and vegetables. The consortium of merchants sold everything from imported olives and cheese to the finest domestic and imported wine. Whenever she called in her order, it was delivered to her door within twenty-four hours.

"I…" Tamara's retort trailed off when she heard a whining sound. Walking into the bedroom, she stopped when she saw a crate in a corner with a fluffy white puppy in it, standing on its hind legs, front paws pressed against the wire.

Her eyes filled. She turned and smiled at Duncan as tears of joy streaked her face. "You didn't."

He nodded. "Yes, I did. And no matter what happens between us, I won't ask for her back."

Tamara sniffled in an attempt to bring her fragile emotions under control. "You got me a girl?"

"Yes. When I saw her I knew she'd be perfect

for you. Why don't you open the crate and meet Miss Wolcott."

Duncan watched Tamara take tentative steps as she approached the crate. The puppy whined to get out. Tamara went to her knees, sliding back the latch and seconds later she was cradling the wiggling puppy against her breasts.

"She's beautiful, Duncan. Thank you."

"The papers attesting to her pedigree are on the table along with a printout of her vaccinations. The breeder said the cream shading on her chest may or may not disappear. If it does, then she'll be all white as an adult."

Tamara looked at Duncan over her shoulder. "When did she get her shots?"

"I stopped at a vet after I picked her up from the breeder this morning to have her checked out and he said she's in good health. She's three months and weighs three pounds, seven ounces. And she's also paper-trained."

Burying her face in the soft curly coat, Tamara closed her eyes. Her new puppy wouldn't replace Snowflake, but she would love this one as much or more because Duncan had given it to her.

"I just came up with a name for her."

Duncan approached the woman who'd managed to turn his life upside-down within the span of a week. Going to his knees, he wrapped his arms around both Tamara and the puppy.

"What are you naming her?"

Tamara raised her head, her gaze fusing with his. "Duchess Wolcott-Gilmore."

His gaze dropped to her parted lips. "Shouldn't it be Gilmore-Wolcott?"

"No, darling. If Angelina Jolie and Brad Pitt can name their children Jolie-Pitt, then I can name my baby Wolcott-Gilmore."

"Easy, mama," he crooned, "I didn't mean to insult your baby girl."

Rising slightly, Tamara pressed her mouth to his, deepening the kiss when his tongue slipped between her lips. A swathe of heat swept over her, and she moaned as a ball of desire exploded between her legs. It was merely a kiss, but she felt as if she lay naked with his hard sex inside her.

The chiming of a bell echoed throughout the condo, signaling a bark and wavering sound from Duchess that resembled howling.

Duncan stood up, reached down and helped Tamara gently to stand. "That must be the food."

He crossed the room and pushed a button on the intercom near the bedroom door. "Yes?" he said into the speaker.

"I've got a delivery from Gotham City Market."

"Come on up." He punched another button, disengaging the lock on the outer door. Shifting, he saw Tamara with Duchess cradled to her chest, staring at him. "How much is the bill?"

"Six hundred and seventy-eight dollars and thirty-nine cents."

"What on earth did you buy? Caviar?"

She smiled. "Yes and a few other things. That's why I told you I'd pay for it."

Duncan pointed a finger. "I told you I'd get it. I always keep cash in the house."

Turning on his heel he walked out of the guest bedroom and into his own where he kept a supply of cash in the event of an emergency. He'd begun the practice after the August 14, 2003, blackout, when he had less than twenty dollars on his person and was unable to access ATMs.

He counted out eight one-hundred-dollar bills and descended the stairs. A close-circuit monitor showed the image of a man in coveralls with Gotham City Market stitched on the pocket and on the front of his cap.

The door opened and the deliveryman pushed three oversized plastic bins on a dolly out of the elevator. "Where do you want me to unload these, mister?"

"Follow me."

Duncan stood numbly by as the bins were emptied and fresh fruit, vegetables and containers and cans of foodstuffs littered the countertop. He smiled when he spied a tiny tin of caviar.

"That's it, mister." The stocky deliveryman, who sported a thick black handlebar mustache, removed an invoice from the pocket of his coveralls.

Duncan handed him the crisp bills. "Keep the change."

"Thanks!"

"You're welcome." He walked the deliveryman to the elevator, waiting until the door closed. Turning a key in a wall switch, Duncan locked the elevator door. Tamara met him as he made his way back to the kitchen. She handed him a book.

"Cooking for Yourself," he mumbled, reading the title aloud. "It looks like interesting reading."

Tamara threaded her fingers through Duncan's free hand. "It looks more intimidating than it actually is," she said, when he gave her a pointed look.

He placed the book on the counter next to some jars of mustard. "Did you order quail eggs to go along with the caviar?"

"Not this time."

Wrapping his arms around her waist as Tamara began sorting through the jars, tins and boxes on the countertop, Duncan eased the hem of her tank top from the waistband of her shorts. "I'm going to enjoy playing house with you."

Tamara closed her eyes and pressed the back of her head to his shoulder, enjoying the feel of his hands on her bare skin. At that moment she didn't want to play house. What she wanted was the real thing.

When they'd been stuck in the elevator she'd told Duncan that she had loved being married. Even so, there was never a time when she'd actually felt like a wife, because she'd become nothing more than a legal companion. She and Edward rarely saw each other, and when they did it wasn't to make love but to talk about their work. That was something she could've done with any man.

Duncan heard the soft hitch in Tamara's breathing when he cupped her breasts. They were full, firm and heavy, like ripened melons. The undeniable magnetism that had been so apparent when they were trapped in the elevator, the vaguely sensuous anticipation felt whenever they occupied the same space, frightened him because he feared losing control.

He'd gone for prolonged periods of time without sleeping with a woman, but now Duncan wanted to make love to Tamara with an intensity that threatened to embarrass him.

"Duncan." His name came out in a fevered whisper when Tamara felt his erection pressing against her hips.

He answered her entreaty, fastening his mouth to the side of her neck. "Baby…I can't…"

Tamara was drowning, sinking deeper and deeper into an abyss of longing that threatened to swallow her whole. She wanted Duncan to take her—right there in the kitchen, throwing caution to the wind.

"Don't move, darling. Please don't move," she pleaded. If he did move then it would be all over and she'd beg him to make love to her.

But he did move. He turned and walked out of the kitchen, leaving her trembling with an intense throbbing that left her wet and shaking. Closing her eyes, she waited for the long-forgotten pleasurable sensation to fade.

Tamara wanted to shower but knew putting away fresh meat, fish and dairy items took precedence. Three-quarters of an hour passed before the freezer section of the refrigerator was filled with wrapped and labeled meat and fish, the refrigerator shelves with dairy, vegetable drawers with fruit and vegetables and pantry shelves with neatly stacked jars, bottles, cans and tins of nonperishable items.

She went upstairs to her bedroom to find Duncan sitting in a chair with the puppy asleep on his lap. Avoiding his eyes, she went over to the weekender resting on a luggage rack and opened it.

"Please put Duchess back in her crate, or she'll get used to someone holding her while she's sleeping."

Duncan didn't move. "I want to make her feel secure in her new environment."

Tamara removed a dress with spaghetti straps and set of underwear from the bag. "I don't want you to spoil her, Duncan."

"What if I spoil you, Tamara?"

"I'm too old to be spoiled."

He ran a finger back and forth over the puppy's ear. "A woman never gets too old for spoiling. All you have to do is ask my aunt. I try and give her whatever she wants because I love her."

Tamara turned and stared at Duncan, her eyes widening when she saw something in his that hadn't been there before. "The difference, Duncan, is that you don't love me."

A slow smile tilted the corners of his mouth—a very sexy mouth that did things she'd forgotten the existence of to her body. "Do you know that for certain?"

A rush of heat slammed her face, making it hard for Tamara to think or to draw a normal breath. "No—no, I—I don't know for certain," she stammered.

Duncan pushed to his feet, still cradling the puppy. She wasn't certain, but he was. He didn't love Tamara Wolcott. However, he knew beyond a shadow of a doubt that he was falling in love with her. He couldn't right the wrongs of her ex-husband, but he'd promised himself that he would try to make whatever time they had together fun and memorable.

"Duchess and I will be on the terrace."

Tamara's jaw dropped when Duncan opened the sliding door to the terrace, stepped out and closed it behind him. Walking over to the wall of glass, she closed the floor-to-ceiling sheers then the silk drapes, closing out the sunlight and the image of the man and *her* dog reclining on a chaise.

She knew her feelings for Duncan were intensifying with each telephone call and whenever they shared the same space. She wasn't certain how he felt about her, but she was more than cognizant of her feelings for him. Tamara Wolcott was falling hopelessly and inexorably in love with Duncan Gilmore.

Chapter 10

Tamara, knowing she couldn't put off the inevitable, joined Duncan on the terrace. She smiled. He lay on the chaise with Duchess between his legs. The puppy was still asleep.

Duncan saw movement out of the corner of his eye and turned to find Tamara only a few feet away. "Come join us." He gently lifted Duchess with one hand, while patting the cushion with the other. He opened his legs wider. "Sit here."

Tamara sat down, swinging her legs over the chaise and pressing her back to Duncan's chest. Peering over her shoulder, she winked at him. "May I have *my* dog?" He handed her the puppy, who whined softly before settling down on her lap and promptly going back to sleep.

"Now, who's spoiling her highness?" Duncan crooned in Tamara's ear.

"I can because she's my baby."

Resting his chin on her bared shoulder, he inhaled the sensual subtlety of her perfume. "You're a hypocrite, darling."

"No, I'm not."

"You can spoil Duchess, yet you won't permit me to spoil you."

"No man has ever spoiled me," Tamara retorted.

"Not even your father?"

"No, Duncan, not even my father. That's not to say Daddy doesn't love me or my sisters. He's from the old school that a wife and mother's responsibility is taking care of the home and rearing children.

"Most times he could be found in his study either preparing lectures or exams. My sisters and I learned early on never to bother him when the door was closed. I remember the time when I sat on the floor outside his study waiting for him to open the door to show him my report card. When he finally opened it hours later he asked how long I'd been waiting. When I told him I'd waited more than two hours to show him that I'd made the high honor roll, he told me I could always interrupt him if it pertained to school. Of course, my sisters were pissed that I'd been granted special privileges so they cranked up the bitch meter to turn Daddy against me."

"Did it work?"

"No because Daniel Wolcott despised tattling and they knew it."

"Are you estranged from your sisters?"

"No," Tamara admitted truthfully. "It's different now that we're adults. Tiffany is the middle child and she runs hot and cold. The only thing I'm going to say is that I pray for her husband. Renata and I have grown closer over the years. I was at her house earlier this week because she was having an emotional meltdown."

"Is that why you asked me about a divorce attorney?"

Tamara stared at the throngs along Chelsea Piers. It was late afternoon and there was a steady stream of tourists disembarking from tour buses coming to take in the sights of the city.

"Yes," she said after an interminable pause. "She has proof that her husband has been cheating on her."

"Has she confronted him?"

"I told her not to until she speaks to a lawyer. She doesn't want to use the one she has because he's a family friend. I don't want Renata to end up screwed like I was."

"Does she have children?"

"She has two teenage girls. I know it's going to

destroy them when they find out their parents are breaking up. They adore their father."

Duncan wrapped his arms around Tamara's waist. "Do you think there's the possibility she might consider marital counseling? There's always a reason why men and women cheat."

"Have you ever cheated on a woman?"

"No. Are you asking because you think I'd cheat on you, Tamara?"

"No."

"Well, I wouldn't."

"Has a woman ever cheated on you?" Tamara felt the strong, steady beating of Duncan's heart against her back.

"Yes."

"What did you do when you found out?" she asked.

"I stopped seeing her."

There came a beat. "I can't imagine what Renata is going through because I've never been faced with a cheating partner. I take that back," Tamara retracted quickly. "I had a pretend boyfriend in junior high who took one of my friends to the movies. Of course, my so-called best girl couldn't wait to call me up to tell me. I suppose they expected me to go off on him but I decided ignoring him was better."

Duncan laughed. "Pretend boyfriends don't count. What about high school?"

"I didn't have one date in high school."

"You're kidding!"

"No, Duncan, I'm not kidding. I wasn't willing to put out, so I became persona non grata. The alienation was overwhelming, but I managed to cope by taking as many AP courses that I could. I graduated at sixteen and by the time I entered college I was already a junior."

Duncan whistled. "You're really a brainiac."

"Not really."

"You shouldn't have to apologize about being smart. Embrace it."

Her smile was dazzling. "Okay. Tamara Wolcott is smart!"

"There you go. Was your ex your first lover?"

"No. I met a film-school student and we started out as friends. One night we had too much wine and ended up in bed together. I don't know who was more shocked, because it was the first time for both of us."

"Blind leading the blind," Duncan whispered.

"That's mean, Duncan. I'm certain the first time you slept with a woman you were no saint."

He sobered quickly. "You're right."

"Enough sex talk. I think it's time for you to begin your lessons."

Duncan pressed a kiss to the nape of her neck. "Baby, can we begin tomorrow?"

Tamara emitted a soft moan. "Why are you putting off the inevitable?"

"What's that?"

"Learning to cook," she countered.

"Oh, man. I should've never agreed to this cooking lesson business."

Shifting so as not to disturb the puppy, Tamara stared at Duncan. The lenses of his glasses had darkened in the light, not permitting her to see the emotion lurking in the depths of his eyes.

"If you don't want to do it, then I'll take my baby and go home."

"No, please stay."

Her gaze dropped to the lines of tension ringing his mouth. "What if I cook tonight and you watch? We can have a simple meal with candlelight and music."

Duncan grimaced. "I don't think I have any candles."

"Yes, we do. When I called in the grocery order I had them include candles and flowers."

He kissed her again, this time along the column of her neck. "There's no way I'm going to let you go."

There's no way I'm going to let you go.

His pronouncement lingered with Tamara as he seated her at the dining room. The overhead chandelier was dimmed to its lowest setting and the soft light from vanilla-scented pillar candles cast flattering shadows over the bone china, crystal stemware and silver place settings. Music flowed from speakers concealed throughout the first floor.

Rounding the table, Duncan sat opposite Tamara. "I can't believe you cooked everything in half an hour," he said, filling a glass with a dry white wine.

The actual cooking time had been about thirty-five minutes. Prep time, which included cracking the hen's breastbone in order to make the bird lie flat when broiled, had been about ten minutes. Then she had placed the seasoned hen in the refrigerator for an hour to marinate in extra-virgin olive oil, coarsely ground pepper and sea salt.

"Preparation and marinating the bird takes up most of the time," Tamara explained. "Whenever I work days I usually prepare whatever I'm going to cook the night before. That way, when I get home, all I have to do is either broil it or put it in the microwave. I eat, clean up the kitchen and have the rest of the evening to relax."

"That's easy, but not as easy as ordering in."

"Eating out and ordering in isn't healthy for you unless in moderation."

Duncan winked at her. "Yes, Dr. Wolcott."

"I'm serious, Duncan."

He sobered quickly. "I know, Tamara. Cooking and cleaning are not my areas of expertise. I have a plaque in my office that reads Numbers Rule. Numbers are my little friends. They don't talk back." He raised his wineglass. "Cheers to the cook."

Tamara raised her glass, touching it to his. "Cheers."

She took a sip of wine, holding it in her mouth for several seconds before letting it slide down the back of her throat. The wine was excellent. She picked up her knife and fork, cutting into the browned and crunchy skin of the hen. "I'm willing to bet if I order a complete blood workup on you you'd be surprised at the results."

"That's where you're wrong, Tamara. I just had a complete physical, including blood work and I'm pleased to report that I'm quite healthy."

"Do you work out?" She wanted to know, because for someone who probably spent hours sitting behind a desk his body was rock-hard.

"Yes. There's a gym set up on the street level of the brownstone that all the building employees use. There are treadmills, elliptical and rowing machines."

Tamara stared at her dining partner. No wonder he didn't have an ounce of fat on his lean frame.

"How often do you work out?"

"At least three to four times a week. I usually go to work in sweats, work out, and then take a shower at the office. I keep a supply of shirts, ties, suits and underwear at the office to change into, along with grooming supplies."

"That's really convenient. I signed on with a gym in my neighborhood but I hardly ever get to use it. After working twelve straight hours all I want is to go home and sleep."

Duncan drained his glass, then refilled it and Tamara's. "You don't need a gym. Your body's perfect." He stared at his dining partner over the rim of his glass. Everything was perfect: the meal, the candlelight, the softly playing music as a backdrop. Even the white bouquet was perfect. When he'd asked Tamara what the flowers were she'd identified them as violets, lily-of-the-valley and sweet peas.

The only flowers he was familiar with were roses, tulips and hydrangeas because they were his aunt's favorites. A wry smile touched his mouth. Within days of meeting Tamara he'd sent her flowers. Unfortunately, it hadn't happened with Kali because she was allergic not only to flowers but also to perfume. Whenever they were together he'd had to forego wearing aftershave and cologne.

He didn't cook and neither had Kali. He only discovered that after he'd had the kitchen renovated. He'd wanted the gourmet kitchen to be a surprise, but the joke was on him when his fiancée announced she didn't want to learn to cook. Why should she when she was going to marry a wealthy man?

Her explanation had made Duncan take thought as to why Kalinda had pressured him to propose marriage. When he'd broached the subject she'd apologized profusely, declaring she would marry him even if he'd been a pauper.

"Duncan, are you all right?"

He blinked as if coming out of a trance. "Yes. Why?"

"I just asked you about the plans for your party?"

"It's…they're good. I'm letting a friend's wife

handle everything. She's an event and wedding planner. How's it going with your father's birthday celebration?"

"We've decided to have it at the Hudson Terrace."

"The Hudson Terrace on Forty-Sixth Street?"

"Yes. Are you familiar with it?"

Raw hurt glittered in Duncan's eyes. "Yes. I'm quite familiar with it. It's a beautiful place." He and Kalinda had contracted to have their wedding and reception at the opulent Hudson River venue with its all-season rooftop lounge.

"I'd like to invite you to be my date for that night." Tamara gave Duncan a lingering look when he didn't respond. "If you don't want to come with me, then I'll ask Rodney."

"Who the hell is Rodney?"

She bit on her lip to keep from laughing. Duncan sounded like a jealous lover. "He's my roommate."

"What's the deal with you and your roommate? Are you sleeping with him, Tamara?"

"What!" The word exploded from her mouth.

"You know you heard what I said."

"I heard it, but I can't believe you'd ask me something like that."

"And why not, Tamara?"

"Because it's disgusting. Do you think I'd invite you to get into bed with me if I was sleeping with another man who happens to be living with me?"

"I don't know, Tamara. You tell me."

"I like you, Duncan—a lot. And to me that translates into sleeping with one man at a time."

Duncan rested his elbows on the table. "There's something wrong with your translation because we are *not* sleeping together."

Her fist came down, rattling china and silver. "But I do want to sleep with you," she shouted.

As soon as the words were out Tamara knew she couldn't retract them. She'd said what lay in her heart, what she'd felt from the time she'd sat on the floor of the elevator and Duncan had put his arm around her.

Pushing back his chair, Duncan came around the table and held out his hand. He watched Tamara staring at his hand. He counted slowly, telling himself that if she didn't take his hand when he got to ten then he'd walk away from her for the second time that day. He was certain she heard his sigh of relief when she placed her palm on his. His hand closed over hers as he helped her to her feet.

Tamara closed her eyes when she found herself cradled against the chest of a man who'd quietly ingratiated himself into her life. Whenever he touched or kissed her she was reminded that she was a woman—a woman with strong passions she'd repressed and denied.

Before she had a chance to react, she found herself swept up in his arms as he carried her across the living room to the staircase. So many thoughts crowded her mind, so many questions she wanted to ask, but she found herself completely mute. Wrapping her arms around Duncan's neck, she buried her face against his shoulder.

I want him.

I need him.

The statements played like a litany, burning a tattoo on her brain. Tamara didn't know why she wanted Duncan Gilmore when it hadn't been that way with any other man—and that included her ex-husband.

With Edward it had been more of a need for his approval. Subconsciously, she'd replaced her father with Edward: if she excelled then she would get the praise she felt she so rightly deserved. It wasn't about sex because it'd taken them two years to sleep together, and they'd only done so when she'd become his wife.

However, it would be different with Duncan because *she* was different. Tamara wasn't curious about sex and she wasn't seeking his approval. Duncan had come to Tamara at the very best time of her life.

She was secure in her career, solvent, and she knew what she wanted. For the first time in her life she was in complete control. The insecurities she'd harbored as a little girl and an adolescent were gone.

Tamara knew she would never wear a single-digit dress size, and she had accepted that reality. It'd taken three decades for her to learn to love herself, because in the past she'd learned not to expect loving from others.

The love she'd felt for her college boyfriend had been more of a dependency. He was her first lover and she'd wanted to hold onto that significance. In her relationship with Edward he'd become that father figure—someone she could go to for wise counsel. She'd viewed him as her teacher *and* her protector.

The man cradling her to his chest wasn't a father figure, but an equal. Duncan Gilmore was a man who treated and respected her as a woman. He was gentle, generous, and above all, she trusted him.

Duncan prayed that what was about to happen wasn't a dream and then when he awoke, he wouldn't be in bed alone fantasizing about what he'd wanted to do and share with Tamara Wolcott.

He'd met Tamara less than two weeks ago, and during that time he had experienced a gamut of emotions he hadn't known existed. The initial attraction had been purely physical. The image of her standing in the elevator buttoning a shirt that exposed more than it concealed was branded into his brain.

The first thing that had shocked him was the deep gold-brown color of her skin, then the look of surprise in her dark slanting eyes when she realized he could see her breasts through a white lace bra. Tamara was too startled to notice, but he hadn't been able to control an instantaneous erection. Yes, he'd experienced them as a teenage boy, but not as a sexually experienced man.

The short time they were trapped together in the elevator had proved to Duncan that Tamara Wolcott was unique, that his reaction to her was more than infatuation. She'd had her share of ups and downs, good and bad, yet in the end she had emerged stronger, more secure.

He'd had to deal with the loss of two women in his life, but instead of dealing with his grief and moving on he'd allowed it to drag him down emotionally. He'd put up a shield: not gotten involved, not permitted a woman to get too close. When he found a woman wanting or asking for more, he preferred to walk away.

But Duncan didn't want to walk away from Tamara. Not only did he want her in his bed, he also wanted her in his life. What she didn't know was that he was willing to give her anything she wanted that was in his power to give.

Tamara would never replace Kalinda because she wasn't Kalinda. His love for his dead fiancée had come out of a need to protect. What he was beginning to feel for Tamara was an aching need for fulfillment.

Professional success had come easily—too easily, but it was personal success that was always elusive. He'd dated women of different races and ethnic

backgrounds, hoping to find a sense of contentment.
At first he'd enjoyed the variety, but after a while
he'd found himself bored with having to mentally
switch gears to adjust to not his criteria but theirs.

Then he'd met Kalinda Douglas. At first he'd
found her withdrawn, reticent, like a frightened
child. Once she'd opened up to him, Duncan knew
she needed rescuing. What he hadn't known at the
time was that it was her overprotective, controlling
parents she needed to be saved from, not herself.

And he'd appointed himself her knight in shining
armor, her guardian angel. He'd set up a bank
account for her so she could withdraw money to buy
what she'd deemed *forbidden*. The first time she
bought a bra and panty set from Victoria's Secret
she called him at his office to say she had something
to show him. He'd given her a key to his condo, so
when he walked in later that night he found her
sprawled across the bed in a black lace thong panty
and demi-bra that had revealed more than it had
concealed. That had been the first time he'd made
love to her, and it was the time he'd realized Kalinda
was not a virgin.

Duncan knew Tamara wasn't a virgin; she hadn't
professed to be one. There was no doubt she wasn't
as sexually experienced as he, which meant he had
to go slow with her. She'd admitted to sleeping with
a bumbling boy and with a man old enough to be
her father, and he found that almost laughable.

He'd known from their first kiss that Tamara Wolcott was a sexy, sensual woman, and each time he touched or kissed her he'd felt her response. She wanted more and he wanted much, much more.

Walking into his bedroom, he placed Tamara on the bed. Reaching down, he took off her shoes. Duncan had closed the sheers over the terrace windows, but not the drapes and the light coming through the delicate fabric from the street provided enough illumination to see the outline of her body. He took off his glasses, leaving them on the bedside table.

He smiled when Tamara raised her arms to welcome him into her embrace. Sinking down to the bed, he supported his weight on his elbows as he lay between her legs.

Slowly, tentatively, he brushed his lips against hers, inhaling the lingering scent of wine on her breath. "I will protect you," he whispered.

Tamara nodded because she couldn't bring herself to speak. She'd known—something in the back of her brain had communicated when she was trapped in the elevator with the well-dressed man— that their lives would be inexorably entwined.

Perhaps her fear of small spaces had prompted her to give him an abbreviated version of her life story, but Duncan had been her rock in that elevator, someone she'd leaned on and relied upon to keep her calm. She was falling in love with him not so much because she needed him as because she wanted him.

Her hands went to his shirt, gathering fabric and pulling it up and over his shoulders. She'd wanted their coming together to be slow, leisurely, but Tamara knew that would have to be another time.

She smiled in the muted darkness when he sat back on his knees to unsnap the waist of his jeans. There were only the sounds of air flowing through the central-airconditioning vents and their breathing, each keeping perfect tempo with the other.

Duncan fumbled with the zipper, and she sat up and brushed his hand away. "Let me do that." Her voice had dropped to a hoarse whisper. The sound of the zipper, the rustle of material and the muffled moan from deep within Duncan's broad chest when Tamara reached through the opening of his boxers to find him hard and heavy were added to the sounds. There was no pretense. She wanted him and she wanted him inside her.

"Don't!" His hoarse cry exploded in the room.

Duncan divested himself of his clothes and shoes, sweeping them off the bed to the floor. When Tamara's hand closed on his sex again he prayed not to spill his passion on the sheets. His hands were shaking as he leaned over to open the drawer in the bedside table. He knew he had to slip on a condom before undressing Tamara or he would go inside her without protection. His hands had steadied enough for him to open the packet and slip the latex over his erection.

Tamara closed her eyes, letting her senses take over. She felt Duncan search for the zipper to her dress. They sighed in unison as it gave way and he was able to ease the dress up and over her head. A slight chill shook her when the cool air kissed her exposed flesh.

Duncan moved over her again, trailing light kisses over her throat, down her breastbone and to her belly. Her hands tightened into fists. He pressed his mouth to the triangle of silk and breathed a kiss there. The heat from his mouth added to the fire that threatened to singe her.

Looping his fingers in the waistband of her panties, Duncan eased them down Tamara's smooth thighs and legs so slowly that it set her teeth on edge. "Please, please," she pleaded shamelessly. He was torturing her.

Duncan knew what she wanted because he wanted the same. Tonight there was to be no prolonged foreplay. He'd waited too long for a woman like Tamara to come into his life. Bracing a hand on each of her knees, he spread them apart as he lowered himself over her prone body.

Tamara smiled. Reaching between their bodies, she grasped his penis, guiding it into her body. Throwing back her head, she bit on her lip as he eased his erection into her celibate flesh.

The soft moans coming from the back of her throat at the slight pain eased; the pain was replaced with a pleasure she'd never known as Duncan established a rhythm that raised tiny flesh bumps all over her body.

Duncan was close, but he wanted to get closer. Sliding his palms under Tamara's hips, he lifted her off the mattress at the same time as she wrapped her legs around his waist. Going to his knees, he pulled her to him, she arched her back in an attempt to get even closer. The sensation of his testicles beating a rhythmic tattoo against her thighs made his erection larger, longer and it became his undoing. He felt the intense tightening in the sac and the burning at the base of his spine. He didn't want it to be over until Tamara climaxed. He lowered her hips, his hands moving up to cover her magnificent breasts.

Tamara gasped when Duncan gently kneaded her breasts. His fingers swept over the nipples until they were as hard as pebbles. Her breathing was coming in deep pants as the throbbing between her thighs intensified. The walls of her vagina contracted, relaxed, then contracted again, each time stronger and with more intensity.

Pulling back slightly in an attempt to delay ejaculating, Duncan plunged deeper, harder. Each time he pulled back, it was a little farther and each time he plunged, it was a little deeper. He took long, measured strokes before quickening them. Beads of sweat dotted his forehead and upper lip.

He felt her contractions squeeze his blood-engorged sex, and Duncan knew he couldn't hold on any longer. Lowering his head, he buried his face against Tamara's neck and groaned, yielding to the burning need that made him crave a woman who'd come into his life when he'd least expected.

Tamara lost count of the orgasms overlapping each other and leaving her unable to move. Even when the moment of ecstasy had passed, she lay motionless. Only the rising and falling of her chest indicated she was still alive.

I love him.

That was her last thought before she succumbed to the sated sleep reserved for lovers.

Chapter 11

Daylight had filtered through the sheers when Tamara opened her eyes to stare at a broad brown back. The ache, albeit pleasurable, between her legs was a reminder of what had happened the night before. She remembered sitting down to dinner, drinking a glass of wine and eating only half her dinner before she and Duncan came upstairs to make love.

I love you. The three words came back and she sat up, pulling up the sheet to cover her breasts. Had she told Duncan that she loved him? *Please no,* she prayed silently.

"Why are you moving around so much?"

Tamara froze. She hadn't realized Duncan was

awake. "I just remembered I have to take care of Duchess."

Duncan rolled over, smiling. "I took care of her already."

Tamara ran a hand over her mussed hair. "When did you take care of her?"

"About an hour ago. I put down clean wee-wee pads, gave her some food and fresh water. When I left her she was chewing on a teething ring."

She gave him a dazzling smile. "Thank you for taking care of my baby."

He lifted his expressive eyebrows. "Don't forget, she's also my baby."

Tamara sucked her teeth at the same time she rolled her eyes. "I don't think so, Duncan Gilmore. You can't give me a dog as a gift and then expect me to share it with you."

Reaching out, Duncan pulled the sheet from her loose grip, his gaze going to what he hadn't been able to see the night before. "Yes, I can," he said, staring at her breasts.

Tamara swatted at his head, deliberately missing him. "No you can't. And stop looking at me like that."

"Like what, baby?"

"Like a pervert."

He licked his lips, then moved with lightning speed when he fastened his mouth to one breast. He caught the nipple between his teeth. "Now, who's a pervert," he mumbled.

Tamara felt the sensation sweep down her body to her vagina when he tightened his grip on her nipple. It wasn't hard enough to hurt, but it turned her on. She gasped when his hand swept up her thigh to find her wet and pulsing with a desire only he could assuage.

She was totally unprepared for the maelstrom and the onslaught of emotions and sensations that assailed her when Duncan released her breast and moved down her body to bury his face between her thighs. Her fingers caught the sheet, holding it in a death grip as her whole body flooded with desire.

She was on fire!

Duncan had awakened her dormant sexuality. His mouth and tongue were relentless, taking Tamara to heights she'd never known. Passion and love radiated from her core to her extremities.

"No more, Duncan," she pleaded. She couldn't take any more because she feared losing herself in what had become a raw act of possession and power.

But Duncan was relentless. It was his intent to wipe away the memory of every other man who'd touched Tamara, any who'd kissed her, and all who wanted her. He wanted to be the last man in her life, and if he no longer existed then she would be left with the memories.

Tamara found the strength to sit up. Pushing against his broad shoulders, she attempted to push his head up, but she wasn't strong enough. Her fingernails biting into the column of his neck did the trick. He glared up at her, and for a brief moment Tamara shrank back. She rested a hand over her throat as if to protect it from the menacing teeth of a predator.

Duncan pounced on Tamara, suckling her breasts. The unbridled turbulence of his passionate assault left her shaking uncontrollably. Love, passion, desire merged, becoming one. The trembling inside her heated her blood and she knew only Duncan could extinguish the fire. She reached for him, finding him hard and ready. His hand closed over hers when he pushed into her heated body.

Time stood still while Duncan made love to Tamara as if it were the last time. Gusts of passion shook them from head to toe, ending in a soaring, uncontrollable moment when they climaxed simultaneously.

The enormity of what they'd done hit Duncan when he withdrew from Tamara's moist warmth. He'd made love to her without using a condom. He felt his heart beating all over his body, and believed he was having a panic attack.

"Tamara!" Her name came out in a strangled cry.

Something in Duncan's voice penetrated the fog of lingering ecstasy, and Tamara sat up quickly. "What's the matter? Talk to me, Duncan!"

He took deep breaths to slow down his respiration, and within seconds it was over. "I'm okay."

Placing a hand over Duncan's chest, Tamara

counted the beats of his heart. It was within the normal range. Smiling, she buried her face between his neck and shoulder. "Talk to me, darling."

"I shouldn't have done that."

"Done what, darling?"

"I didn't use a condom."

Raising her head, Tamara saw the look of distress on his handsome face. "Do you have an STD?"

"No."

"Then what are you so upset about?"

"What if I get you pregnant?"

"And if you did, Duncan? It wouldn't be the end of the world, at least not for me."

His eyes narrowed. "Are you saying you wouldn't have it? You'd abort my baby?"

"Come now, darling. Don't be so melodramatic. Remember, I am doctor. I swore an oath to save a life, not take one."

"That means you'd have it?"

Tamara knew it was time to stop teasing him. "You're not going to get me pregnant because I'm taking a low-dose contraceptive to regulate my periods. My cycle has always been irregular, but even more so the past two years. I would have a flow, then go months without one. At first I thought I was entering early menopause until I had my estrogen level checked. It was within the normal range for my age, so my gynecologist prescribed a low-dose birth control pill."

Duncan didn't know whether to be buoyed or disappointed by Tamara's revelation. He'd told his aunt that he felt ready to become a single father. The only drawback would be delaying the adoption until after he completed the MBA/JD program. He didn't want to adopt a child, then transfer the responsibility of raising his son to a nanny or housekeeper.

He'd want to do all the things with his child he hadn't experienced with his own father. Duncan would teach him to ride a bike, take him to sporting events, visit the zoo and amusement parks, teach him to swim and most importantly help him with his schoolwork, all the while stressing education is the key to success.

Cradling her face in his hands, Duncan gave Tamara a long, penetrating look. "Do you want children?"

Now it was Tamara's turn to discover her heart pounding in a runaway rhythm as she found herself fighting her feelings. She didn't want to need Duncan as much as she did, because after her divorce she'd taken an oath never to want or need another man in her life.

Edward's flaw wasn't that he couldn't be a faithful husband, but that he had a weakness and obsession for gambling—something with which she couldn't compete. He'd taken all of her money, sold the only home she had and even taken her furry companion, only to give it to someone else.

It had taken Tamara a long time to figure out what she had done to Edward to make him resent her and turn on her with such savagery. If she'd snarled at Duncan initially it was because experience had taught her she had good reason to.

"I don't know, Duncan," she said after a pause. "I suppose it would depend on the man."

Duncan lowered his hands and grasped her waist. "Since we never got to finish dinner, I'm going to treat you to breakfast at the Empire Diner."

"No, you're not, Duncan Gilmore. You didn't spend eight hundred dollars on food only to spend more going out to eat," Tamara chastised, smiling. "After we shower we're going down to the kitchen and you are going to make breakfast."

"What if I can't make what I want?"

"What do you want?" she asked.

"Chicken and waffles."

"You're in luck, darling," she crooned. "Of course there's chicken, and waffles. And for someone who admits to barely being able to boil water, you have every appliance and kitchen doodad known to man, so I know you'll have a waffle iron."

"The decorator ordered them."

"Good for him or her, because we're going to rattle some pots."

"Damn," Duncan swore under his breath, "a brother can't catch a break for *nothin'*."

"No, he can't. Not with this sister-girl."

He watched as Tamara moved off the bed and walked toward the bathroom, unable to pull his stunned gaze from her sexy curves. There wasn't one straight line on her tall frame.

Cupping his groin, he swallowed in an attempt to relieve the sudden dryness in his throat. Duncan couldn't believe he wanted her again. Waiting until his erection went down, he slipped off the bed to join the woman who'd unwittingly offered him a second chance at happiness.

Duncan stepped out of the taxi, then extended his hand to Tamara to assist her. He'd had her all to himself for two days and was loath to share her with his friends. They'd cooked together, made love, cooked again and made love again and again. It was as if they couldn't get enough of each other.

Surprisingly he'd taken to cooking like a duck to water, but only after he'd gotten over his initial reluctance. When he'd lived with his aunt there hadn't been a reason to learn to cook because Viola always prepared enough meals every Sunday to last for a week.

Once he entered high school, Duncan bought breakfast at a corner deli before classes and ate school lunches. Dinner was easy because his aunt worked at a neighborhood school and most times she was at home when he arrived.

His ritual changed in college: he'd skip breakfast

and eat lunch at the many delis on Twenty-Third
Street or Park Avenue South. Viola stopped saving
dinner for him. Most times he stayed in the library
studying until the school closed down for the night,
or he shared dinner with classmates or the girl he
was dating at the time.

What saved Duncan was that he rarely ate fast
food. He frequented eating establishments that ad-
vertised selections that were prepared daily.

He'd discovered that Tamara was a firm but patient
teacher. She'd only have to demonstrate carving meat
or filleting fish, slicing and chopping onion and garlic
and peeling veggies and fruit once and he was able
to replicate it. Marinating proved a bit more difficult—he substituted Worcestershire sauce for bal-
samic vinegar because both were the same color. The
length of time for cooking baffled him completely
until Tamara went to the store, returning with digital
thermometers that showed the temperatures for rare,
medium rare and well done meats.

Tamara leaned in closer to Duncan when he rang
the doorbell to the Georgian-style brownstone on
Strivers' Row in the St. Nicholas Historic District.
It was apparent that the boyhood friends from the
projects were living out their dreams. The exterior
of Kyle Chatham's home was exquisite.

The door opened and a tall, dark and breathtak-
ingly handsome man wearing a white golf shirt,
khakis and brown leather sandals beckoned them in.

"Come in, come in, come in," he crooned.

Duncan looped an arm around Kyle's neck. "Thanks for the invite. Kyle, I'd like you to meet Tamara Wolcott. Tamara, this is Kyle Chatham, friend and brother."

Tamara offered her hand, but Kyle ignored it as he leaned over and kissed her cheek. "Welcome."

She met her host's glittering, warm brown slanting eyes. His face was angular with high chiseled cheekbones. There was a sprinkling of gray in his cropped hair. Duncan had told her that Kyle had just proposed to a young woman, and they planned to marry in Puerto Rico on Valentine's Day.

Where, she mused, were men like Duncan Gilmore and Kyle Chatham when she'd been looking for a good black man? She berated herself as soon as the thought entered her head. The answer was she hadn't been looking; she'd spent half her time studying and the other half working long hours, leaving little or no time for a social life.

She'd had more fun cooking and making love with Duncan in the past two days than she'd had since she'd begun medical school. Earlier that morning he'd made breakfast. One of his favorite dishes was eggs Benedict and Tamara had showed him how to substitute smoked salmon for the Canadian bacon, which reduced the sodium content.

Tamara smiled, handing Kyle a cake box. "Here's a little something for dessert."

Kyle took the box, his gaze narrowing. "What's in here?"

"Cannoli," Duncan said. "I know they're your favorite."

"Hot damn, DG, you're the man!" Kyle said, grinning from ear to ear. "Let's go in the back."

"Who's here?" Duncan asked, reaching for Tamara's hand and following Kyle across a spacious foyer with a marble floor into an über-modern kitchen and out a back door to a patio where people milled around talking, eating and drinking.

Tamara breathed a sigh of relief. She'd thought she was going to be overdressed when she'd opted to pair a white shortsleeved silk blouse with a pair of navy linen slacks. The nautical theme was repeated in a pair of blue-and-white striped espadrilles that added an additional three inches to her statuesque figure.

"Micah and Tessa, Ivan with his date, and Jordan and his girlfriend."

Duncan lifted his eyebrows. "I didn't know Jordan had a girlfriend."

"He does and she prepared most of the food. Natasha is in her last year of culinary school."

Duncan caught Kyle's arm, pulling him aside before he began the introductions. "Tamara would like to talk to you about a legal matter."

"What is it, Tamara?"

"I need a referral for a very good divorce attorney."

Kyle stared at the tall, stunning, full-figured woman who could easily pass for a model. He hadn't expected Duncan to bring a date, because it'd been a long time since he'd seen his friend and financial manager with a woman he felt comfortable enough with to introduce to his friends.

"I usually don't handle divorces," Kyle admitted, "but my partner has handled a few. If you want a shark, then Jordan is one of the best. He's the one with his arm around the chef. Come and I'll introduce you to him."

Duncan dropped a kiss on Tamara's hair. "Can I get you something to drink?"

"Iced tea."

She'd said the first thing that came to her mind. It was the middle of the afternoon and with temperatures in the low eighties Tamara wanted to limit her intake of alcohol to avoid dehydration. During the summer, and especially during a prolonged heat wave, people were often admitted to the E.R. suffering from heat exhaustion or dehydration, the result of not increasing their liquid intake or of substituting alcoholic beverages for water.

"Kyle, darling, could you please bring out more ice."

Tamara turned to find an attractive young woman wearing a halter sundress with a revealing décolletage. The sunlight reflected off the diamond on her left hand in a flash of blue and white glints. Her short coiffed hair was nothing short of perfection.

Angling his head, Kyle kissed his fiancée. "I'd like you to meet Duncan's lady. Tamara, this is Ava Warrick. Ava, Tamara Wolcott."

Ava flashed a friendly smile. "It's a pleasure meeting you." She looked around for Duncan. "Where's your boyfriend?"

Tamara blushed. Everyone assumed Duncan was her boyfriend, or was it that obvious from seeing them together? She hadn't draped herself over him, sending out proprietary signals to the other women to stay away. The only sign of affection they'd exchanged was when he'd kissed her hair.

"He's getting me something to drink."

Ava nodded. "Speaking of drinks, if my fiancé doesn't bring out some ice we'll all be drinking warm beverages. What's in the box, Kyle?" she asked without pausing to take a breath.

"Cannoli. Duncan knows they're my favorite dessert."

"Mine, too," Ava confirmed with a Cheshire-cat grin.

Kyle handed her the box. "Please put this in the refrigerator and ask Ivan to bring out the ice. I need to introduce Tamara to Jordan. She needs to discuss some business with him."

Rising on tiptoe, Ava brushed a kiss over Kyle's cheek. "No problem, baby."

Kyle watched his fiancée's retreat, then turned to Tamara, cupping her elbow and steering her over to where Jordan stood next to a tiny dark-skinned woman with a profusion of tiny twists secured on the top her head. She was testing steaks for doneness, the distinctive aroma of grilling meat redolent in the warm air. An outdoor kitchen sat on an expansive deck surrounded by a flower garden with a stone fountain.

"Excuse me, Jordan, but I need a word with you."

Tamara took a good look at the deeply tanned lawyer. Tall and slender, something about his features called to mind the portraits that hung in the hallowed halls of institutions of higher education. His large hazel eyes were sharp, missing nothing. Given his features, she felt Jordan should've had straight blond hair instead of the cropped jet-black curls.

"What's up, Chat?"

"This is Tamara Wolcott. She's a friend of Duncan's, and she needs someone to handle a divorce. Tamara, my law partner, Jordan Wainwright."

Jordan winked at Natasha Parker, who returned the gesture. He guided Tamara to a corner of the deck where they wouldn't be overheard. He pulled out a chair at a table shaded by a large umbrella, seating her, then sat next to her.

"Do you need a divorce attorney for yourself?"

Tamara stared at the toe of his imported slip-on before she glanced up to meet Jordan's steady gaze. "No. It's for my sister."

"Why is she divorcing her husband?"

"She caught him cheating."

Jordan's eyebrows lifted slightly. "She physically caught him cheating?"

"No. She hired an investigator who took photographs of my brother-in-law in a very compromising position with a woman who works in the same company he does."

Grimacing, Jordan bared his teeth. "Nasty. Has she confronted him with the evidence?"

"Not yet. I told her to wait until I talk to an attorney. She has a lawyer, but he's a family friend."

"What does she want, Tamara?"

"She wants a divorce."

"I know that. But what does she want from the divorce? Do they have a house?"

Tamara nodded slowly. "They have a house appraised for almost two million."

Jordan whistled. "What about cars?"

"They have a top-of-the line Benz and a BMW."

"What about children?" Jordan asked, continuing his questioning.

"They have two teenage daughters."

"What are their ages?"

"Thirteen and fifteen."

"I take it your sister and her husband are college-educated."

"Yes. Renata has an MS in education and Robert a Ph.D. in chemistry."

"That means your nieces are entitled to a college education. Does your sister want to keep the house?"

"Yes."

Jordan paused as if he were mulling over what Tamara had told him. "I can get your sister most of what she wants, but she has to know for certain that she wants to divorce her husband."

"I don't understand."

"If I take on your sister's case and then she decides that she wants to reconcile, not only has she wasted her time but also my time. Precious time I can't afford to waste. Your sister should try to get her husband to go to marital counseling with her, so they can air their differences. If she decides she still wants to go through with a divorce, then I'll make him pay through the nose for creeping."

Tamara decided she liked Jordan Wainwright. If she'd had him when she was going through her divorce, there was no doubt she would've been living in the York Avenue co-op with Snowflake. But then, she mused, would she have met Duncan? The odds were she wouldn't have.

"Do you have a business card on you?" she asked Jordan.

"I'm sorry, but I hadn't planned on doing business this weekend. Ask Duncan to give you Kyle's private number at the office. Kyle will patch you through to me."

"Thank you, Jordan."

Leaning over, he pressed a kiss to her cheek. "It's my pleasure."

Tamara stood up, looking around for Duncan. She saw him standing a short distance away, watching her with Jordan. Smiling, she closed the distance between them, and he handed her a tall glass of tea topped off with a sprig of mint.

"What are you drinking?" she asked, touching her glass to his flute filled with a pinkish liquid.

"It's a bellini. Would you like to taste it?"

"It looks like a girlie drink."

Duncan smiled. "If you drink a couple you'll change your mind. Take mine. I'll get another." He took her elbow. "Ivan is doing double duty as bartender." Although his friend was a worse cook than he was, the psychoanalyst was a top-notch mixologist.

Tamara took a sip of the peach-infused cocktail as she followed Duncan over to an area where people had lined up behind a bar, waiting to be served.

Duncan saw Micah standing in front of him. "Where's your wife?"

Micah Sanborn turned. "She's inside lying down."

"What's wrong?"

"She said she was feeling faint."

Duncan and Tamara shared a knowing glance, and she nodded. "Do you mind if Tamara takes a look at her?" He wrapped an arm around Tamara's shoulders. "Micah, this is Dr. Tamara Wolcott. Tamara, Micah Sanborn."

Tamara inclined her head. Micah, like Kyle, was tall, dark and extremely attractive. "I don't have my bag, but I'll take a look at her."

Minutes later, she sat on the side of a bed, taking the pulse of a young woman with a free-style hairdo, catlike brown eyes and bronze skin with a light sprinkling of freckles across the bridge of her nose and on her cheeks. She'd ordered everyone out of the room, closing the door behind.

She smiled at Tessa Sanborn. "Your pulse is normal. How long have you been feeling faint?"

Tessa closed her eyes. "It started yesterday. I was sitting out back and when I went into the house I felt nauseous and then my head started spinning. I think it's the heat."

Tamara leaned closer. "Do you have a problem keeping food down?"

"No. At least I don't think so."

"When was your last period, Tessa?"

She opened her eyes, frowning. "I think it was August. No, it was in July." A rush of color darkened her cheeks.

Tamara bit back a smile. "There is a possibility that you're pregnant." Tessa's mouth opened and closed several times, but nothing came out. "Do you want to know for certain?" Tessa nodded.

Smiling, Tamara patted her hand. "Stay here. I'm going to get a pregnancy test."

"Don't tell my husband what you suspect."

"Of course not. I'll be back."

Tamara opened the door to find Micah waiting outside. "I think it's the heat," she said without a hint of guile. "She needs to rest."

Concern shimmered in the deep-set dark eyes. "Can I go in to see her?"

"Let her rest, Micah. I'll be back to check on her, then you can see her."

She hated deceiving him, but at that moment Tessa Sanborn was her patient and she was bound by doctor-patient confidentiality. Returning to the patio, she found Duncan with a man wearing a colorful Hawaiian shirt, jeans and sandals.

Duncan introduced her to Ivan Campbell, and they exchanged courteous greetings. She noticed the woman clinging to Ivan's arm glaring at her. *I don't want your man, because I have the one I want,* she mused, returning the glare with one of her own.

Tamara offered Ivan a polite smile. "Please excuse me, but I need to speak to Duncan."

"What's the matter?" he asked when they were alone.

"I need you to go to a drug store for me and buy a pregnancy test."

"What!"

"Lower your voice, darling. People are looking at us."

"Are you pregnant?"

She rolled her eyes at him. "Of course not. Please, darling."

Duncan brushed a kiss over her mouth. "Okay. But you owe me."

Smiling, she rested a hand on his smooth cheek. "I owe you."

An hour later Dr. Tamara Wolcott told Micah Sanborn he could see his wife. The test had confirmed that the Kings County ADA and his wedding-planner wife were expecting their first child.

Chapter 12

Tamara sat in the rear of the Town Car, staring out the side window. Tension made it virtually impossible for her to draw a normal breath. She didn't doubt that the surprise celebration for her father would go off well; but how would her family react to seeing her with Duncan?

The past three weeks had changed her life. She went to bed with Duncan and woke up with him. She stopped by her apartment every other day to pick up her mail and check on her prized bonsai plants. Rodney had a prospective buyer for his condo and his real estate agent had given him a mid-October closing date.

She'd given Renata Jordan Wainwright's name and number, and when Renata had informed Robert Powell that she had proof he was having an affair, it was Robert who had pleaded with her not to leave him, saying that he was willing to see a marriage counselor. Although they continued to live under the same roof, Renata refused to let Robert sleep with her until he was tested not once but twice for HIV and STDs.

Tamara found herself growing closer to Renata because they had something in common: deceitful husbands. But unlike Renata, Tamara had moved on; she was down then she was up, crawling slowly but moving.

It had taken her a while to learn to trust a man again, yet it had been easy with Duncan Gilmore. They'd become a couple—in and out of bed. And unofficially they'd become a family with Duchess as their baby. The puppy was growing rapidly and could be let out of her crate for longer and longer periods of time.

During the week Tamara got up early to make breakfast for Duncan. Dinners became a collaborative effort when she and Duncan prepared simple but elegant meals which they ate either in the dining room or on the terrace.

She had four more days before she had to return to the hospital, and even though she was ready to go back to work Tamara was loath to leave Duchess. The bichon frise had become her constant companion, following her everywhere. Tamara took the puppy with her whenever she returned to the East Village to check on her apartment. Duchess knew she was going out whenever she saw her leash or the carrier that cost as much as some designer handbags.

"What are you thinking about?"

Duncan's velvet baritone pulled Tamara out of her reverie. Turning her head, she smiled at him. He looked wonderful in a dark suit, white shirt and a bluish-gray silk tie. It had taken her more than two hours to choose an outfit for the evening. She'd finally decided on a feminine tuxedo with a black pencil skirt, a jacket with a shawl collar and a gray silk vest that doubled as a blouse. Her shoes matched her blouse, the silk-covered slingbacks putting her above the six-foot mark.

"I'm mentally preparing myself to go back to work."

Duncan stared at the sophisticated hairstyle Tamara had affected. She'd explained that she had her hair set on large rollers before she went under the dryer. Then she had to endure the heat from a blow dryer and brush to lift and smooth her hair until it moved as if taking on a life of its own. She admitted that she preferred the curly style because she didn't have to deal with the blow dryer or cover her hair at night to keep it from frizzing.

He wasn't partial to any particular hairstyle because he'd like Tamara Wolcott even if she shaved her head. Tamara was unlike any other woman he'd known. She was strong, independent, traits he'd come to admire in a woman. The women in his past had exhibited a neediness that he'd found appealing because it permitted him to take care of them.

But Tamara didn't need taking care of—she needed him to love her. She hadn't asked him to love her; she didn't even ask if he liked her. He'd had to tell Kali every day that he loved her or she would sulk or pout for weeks on end. After a while it'd become an automatic response: "Yes, Kali, I love you."

Not only did he like Tamara, but he loved her. It was a gentle love he found comforting, soothing. The times when they went to bed and did not make love they talked—about anything and everything. What he found puzzling was that they never talked about themselves. It was as if that topic was taboo.

He knew of the men in her life, but he hadn't told her about Kalinda. To talk about his fiancée would dredge up guilt—guilt that he hadn't trusted Kali to tell him the truth. Guilt that he'd professed to love her when in fact he was always looking for an excuse to end their relationship.

There were times when Duncan didn't know whether she was lying because she'd become so proficient a liar that even though he saw the truth he refused to acknowledge it. He should've known something was wrong when she'd revealed that she was not a virgin—but only after they'd slept together the first time. When he'd confronted her, she'd cried, saying she didn't want him to think less of her because she'd slept with another man. Little did she know that he'd had no wish to become involved with the clingy virgin persona she had perfected to an art form.

What she hadn't lied about was her upbringing. Her controlling mother and tyrannical father had made it impossible for her to have a life of her own. Once Duncan put an engagement ring on her finger, the elder Douglases eased their grip somewhat, but no matter how late Kali stayed out, she still had to go home to sleep in her own bed. He'd paid a car service a small fortune to take her home.

"Do you miss the hospital?"

Tamara wrinkled her nose. "A little bit."

"When are you taking a vacation again?"

"Probably next spring. I have a lot time coming to me."

"I usually take off the last two weeks in April. Tax season begins the first week in January and by April fifteenth my staff is close to burnout. Aside from regular holidays it's the only time I shut down the office completely."

"What if emergency calls come in?" Tamara asked.

"The building receptionists take messages when we don't pick up."

Reaching over, Tamara placed her hand over Duncan's. "I've never been to your office."

"I should've taken you there the day we went to Kyle's cookout."

She thought about the party Duncan was hosting for Kyle and Ava that was scheduled for the day after tomorrow. Tessa Sanborn, one-third owner of Signature Event Planners and Signature Bridals was handling everything from mailing out invitations to contracting a caterer. Tessa's floral-designer sister would deliver bouquets of Ava's favorite flowers and renowned wedding-cake designer Faith McMillan would provide the dessert.

"A good thing about going back to the hospital is that I won't have to work a twelve-hour shift anymore. I don't want to think of leaving Duchess alone for that long."

"You can leave her at my place," Duncan volunteered.

"I'm not going home just to turn around and come to your place to take care of her, Duncan."

"It wouldn't be a problem if you move in with me. As it is we're practically living together."

"We're not living together. What I do is sleep over at your place."

"It's all the same, Tamara."

"No, it's not, Duncan. You have your apartment and I have mine, which gives me the option of sleeping at my own place any time I want."

Duncan went still. Tamara talking about having options spoke volumes. "Do you really think I'd ask you to move in with me, then put you out if we have a disagreement?"

"I don't know what to think," Tamara retorted. "All I know is that I don't want to make the same mistake twice."

"You had no way of knowing when you married your ex that it was going to end the way it did."

"You're right, Duncan. But I promised myself that I would never permit myself to get caught up in a similar position again. Thanks for the offer, but I can't live with you."

A silence descended on the car, blanketing the occupants on the rear seat like a weighted shroud. Tamara wanted Duncan to understand her stance; however, she didn't plan to debate the issue with him. After all, she was the one who'd been made practically homeless even though it'd been her decision to move out of the apartment she'd shared with Edward.

Although she'd been wronged, not once had Edward apologized for taking her money. He'd even had the audacity to say he'd spent *their* money. Her comeback was if it was *their* money, then the co-op was also *theirs*, and she wanted him to sell it and give her half. Edward had smiled and told her that if and when he did sell the apartment she would never get a penny from it. It had been this pronouncement that had prompted her to move out.

Edward Bennett had drawn the proverbial line in

the sand, challenging her to cross it. Tamara had known that if she continued to live with him it would've ended badly. She hadn't been willing to jeopardize her career and her freedom in order to live under the same roof as a man whom she had believed would love and protect her.

"I am not your ex-husband," Duncan spat out.

"You're so right about that, Duncan," Tamara countered.

"Then why are you treating to me as if I were?"

Withdrawing her hand, Tamara shifted to look out the window again. The driver hadn't gone more than two blocks in the last five minutes. Traffic had come to a standstill.

"You don't look like Edward, Duncan, neither do you sound like him. And that means I'd never confuse you with him. My decision to keep my place is not about you. It's about *me* and what makes me feel secure."

Duncan felt a shiver of annoyance shake him to the core. Kalinda couldn't move in with him unless they were married. Meanwhile Tamara, who wasn't faced with those restrictions or limitations, didn't want to live him when that was exactly what she'd been doing the past month.

He didn't want to argue with Tamara because there wouldn't be a winner. Both would be losers if something was said that they'd never be able to retract. He also knew it was unrealistic to expect a relationship in which both partners agreed on everything, but Duncan detested confrontation and sought to avoid it at all costs.

"I'm sorry I brought it up. I won't ask you again."

Tamara closed her eyes as the heat of tears pricked the back of her eyelids. She'd fallen in love with Duncan, loved him enough to marry him—if he asked—but the memory of packing her clothes and books and having a moving company come to put them in storage until she found a permanent home still lingered along the fringes of her mind.

Yes, she was paying an obscene amount of money to rent an apartment that would never really be hers, yet it was still hers. It was a place where, when she put the key in the lock and opened the door, she knew that everything inside belonged to her. As long as she mailed off her check to the landlord each month she was assured of having a place to eat and sleep.

Her accountant had advised her to buy a condo or co-op because she needed a tax write-off. Every year she said she would, but with her long working hours she never seemed to find the time to contact a real estate agent.

"Thank you, Duncan."

"You're welcome, Tamara."

The sound of police sirens rent the air and motorists maneuvered in an attempt to give the emergency vehicles the right of way. Tamara glanced at her watch, groaning inaudibly. She had to get to the restaurant by six-thirty because her mother had confirmed that she and her husband would arrive at seven.

"Duncan, let's walk the rest of the way." They were at Fortieth and the restaurant was on Forty-Sixth Street.

"Are you sure you can walk that far in your heels?"

She smiled. "If I can dance in them, then I can walk in them."

Duncan tapped on the partition separating them from their driver. "We're going to get out here. You can pick us up at the Hudson Terrace at eleven."

The driver put the limo in Park, got out and opened the rear door. He helped Tamara out, then nodded to Duncan as he emerged. "I'll be waiting at eleven."

Taking Tamara's hand, Duncan guided her through the idling cars to the sidewalk amid whistles and crude comments from several male drivers. He knew they were directed at Tamara. She was stunning in the feminine tuxedo. Each time she took a breath the soft swell of her breasts rose and fell above her blouse's revealing décolletage.

He'd been hard-pressed not to stare at her long legs in the heels when she came down the staircase. He'd asked himself over and over how he had gotten so lucky as to have found a woman whose beauty matched her intelligence.

When she'd asked him to buy a pregnancy test

it was the first time he'd seen her in the role of physician. And when Tessa had rejoined everyone on the patio and announced that she and her husband were expecting their first child, the smile on her face was dazzling. Gasps, then silence ensued as she thanked Dr. Wolcott for her quick and accurate diagnosis. A feeling of pride had filled him when he'd realized Dr. Wolcott was his, that she was actually his.

Duncan knew he had turned an emotional corner when 9/11 came and went without him picking up the telephone to call Kalinda's parents. Perhaps, he'd thought, they were ready to move on and so was he. He'd never forget the woman he'd asked to share his name and his future, but that was his past.

Cradling Tamara's hand in the bend of his elbow, he smiled at her. "You look marvelous," he crooned in a dead-on Billy Crystal imitation.

"And you are crazy," she said, laughing.

Releasing her hand, he wrapped an arm around her waist, pulling her closer. "You should know by now that I'm crazy about you."

"That's okay as long as you don't *go* crazy."

"Will you treat me, baby, if I do?"

"I'm an E.R. physician, not a psychiatrist. But I can get you some drugs that'll make you feel good."

"You're the only drug I'll ever need, Dr. Wolcott. Making love with you is better than any illicit substance."

She gave him a sidelong glance. "What do you know about illicit substances?"

Duncan's expression stilled, growing serious. "Unfortunately, too much. A lot of the kids that Ivan and Kyle and I knew got hooked on drugs and they're either dead or in jail. A few managed to kick the habit, but not enough. I ran into a man the other day who'd lived in my building and I didn't recognize him, but he recognized me. The man's only thirty-five, but he didn't have a tooth in his mouth, and he looked old enough to be my father.

"He broke down and cried when he told me that he'd just been paroled after spending eighteen years in prison for armed robbery and assault with a deadly weapon. He has a son, but his baby's mother won't let him see him because she told the boy that his father died years ago. He has a parole officer, but what he needs is a social worker to advocate for him. I gave him my business card, telling him to contact me in a week. Meanwhile Ava is talking to his parole officer to see what services he needs."

"Does he have a place to live?"

"Yes. He's staying with a cousin, but it's only temporary. When I mentioned him to Ivan and Kyle they talked about creating a position for him, even if it's only part-time."

"What can he do?"

"Not much. We discussed bringing him in as maintenance/gofer even though we have a contract with a cleaning company. We try to hire the Harlem residents, because people who work in their own communities tend to spend their money there."

"Is he in rehab?"

"No. He went cold-turkey while incarcerated. I contacted a local dentist and set up an appointment for him to get a set of dentures. He's so conscious of not having any teeth that he refuses to smile."

"You guys are incredible, Duncan."

"No, we're not, Tamara. Kyle, Ivan and I were the luckier ones who managed not to succumb to drug use, dropping out of school, committing crimes or making babies. We had nothing to do with how we turned out. It had everything to do with our parents. Kyle and Ivan grew up with both parents, but my single mother was not to be played with. All she had to do was look at me and I got it together. Even when I went to live with my aunt I still couldn't get away with anything. Aunt Viola told me that if I couldn't follow her rules, then I could always hit the bricks. That meant living in a group home where I would've given myself a week either to survive or get my brains kicked out. Given the choices, I opted to follow the rules. I told my aunt about you, by the way, and she wants you to come for Sunday dinner."

"This Sunday?"

"Yes, this Sunday."

"Duncan, do you realize this entire weekend will be devoted to non-stop socializing? We have my dad's party tonight, Kyle and Ava's party on Saturday and dinner with your aunt on Sunday."

"The summer season is over, so it should be quiet until the Christmas season."

"Will Ivan bring the girl who came with him to Kyle's cookout?"

"I don't know. Why are you asking, Tamara?"

"I don't know whether it's my imagination, but she gave me the nastiest looks whenever I talked with Ivan. I was one step from telling her that I didn't want her man, because I happen to like the one I have thank you very much."

Attractive lines fanned out around Duncan's eyes when he smiled. "To be honest, I've never seen Ivan with the same woman for more than a month or two. I think he has commitment issues."

"We all have issues, Duncan."

"You're right, baby. We all have issues."

Tamara still wrestled with her issues; Duncan was talking about Christmas while she refused to plan beyond the upcoming month. She thought it ironic that he'd grown up in an inner-city housing project but had been better adjusted at twenty-one than she'd been at the same age.

She'd grown up in the suburbs with sprawling homes set on manicured lawns. Most of the kids in her classes came from two-parent homes and getting cars for seventeenth birthdays was the norm rather than the exception.

Not to say there wasn't drug use, because in some communities it reached pandemic proportions, but the difference was it wasn't as overt. If a student was found to be using, his parents sent him to private rehab instead of to the community-based programs. Some communities had their own police forces whose members called parents so their kids would never see the inside of a cell or courtroom.

The "hot" girls who found themselves in trouble had two options: abortion or going away to a "boarding school" where they delivered their babies and gave them up for adoption. The few who chose to keep their babies became pariahs despite the changing attitudes toward unwed teenage mothers.

Tamara and Duncan walked the rest of the way in silence, and she sucked in a deep breath when they arrived at the canopied entrance of the Hudson Terrace. They were directed to the private room where family, friends and colleagues of Daniel Wolcott had gathered to celebrate his big six-o.

Renata spied her first. She closed the distance between them, balancing herself in a pair of Jimmy Choo stilettos. Tamara smiled. One thing she could say about the Wolcott girls was they flaunted their height. Five-foot-eight-inch Renata and Tiffany and Tamara at five-ten all favored very high heels. Renata had taken Tamara's advice and had put back on the weight she'd lost. Another ten pounds and she would be perfect.

The two sisters exchanged air kisses. "You look absolutely incredible, Tami. I never realized you had a smoking-hot body until now, because I'm so used to seeing you in pants and oversized T-shirts."

"It's either scrubs or sweats." Turning, she beckoned to Duncan. "I want you to meet someone."

Renata went completely still as she stared at the man who'd come with her sister. "Oh…my…word," she whispered. "Where did you find *that?*" she crooned sotto voce.

"It's a long story." Tamara held out her hand to Duncan, who took it and dropped a kiss on her fingers. "Duncan, I'd like you to meet my sister, Renata Powell. Renata, Duncan Gilmore."

Renata extended a limp wrist to Duncan, all the while grinning like a Cheshire cat. "I'm charmed."

He stared at her under lowered lids. "Same here, Renata."

The facial resemblance between the two sisters was remarkable, but Duncan found that Renata lacked Tamara's overt sensuality. He couldn't believe he'd just met the woman who'd made Tamara's childhood hell. Groaning inwardly, he saw Renata's clone coming to join them. Now he knew why the sisters had taunted Tamara: they were jealous of her.

Tamara rested her hand on the sleeve of Duncan's navy blue silk-and-wool-blend suit jacket. "This is my other sister, Tiffany Martin. Tiffany, I'd like you to meet my very good friend, Duncan Gilmore."

Tiffany rested her hands on her hips rather than shake Duncan's hand. Resentment glittered in her slanting dark eyes. "Are you also a doctor?"

"No. One doctor in the family is enough."

Renata, resplendent in a black Carolina Herrera silk-tulle-and-chiffon dress exchanged a look with Tiffany. "Are you two hiding something?"

"No," Tamara answered truthfully.

Tiffany crossed her arms under her breasts. "I think I know what it is. Tamara and her *man* are probably living together, because Mother says whenever she calls Tamara she can never reach her. She has to wait days for Tamara to get back to her. You should learn how to access your voice mail, sister dear."

"I don't have to, *sister dear,* because I don't have to check in with anyone, and that includes Mother *and* my man!"

Renata rounded on her sister. "Tiff, please. Not tonight. Let's not ruin it for Daddy."

Tiffany's mouth twisted into a sneer. "Since when did you decide to take her side?"

"I told you, not tonight. For that matter," Renata continued, "I'm done talking about Tamara. Tami, would you and Duncan like to see how the banquet manager set up everything?"

Tamara smiled. "Of course. Tiffany, are you coming with us?"

Tiffany hesitated, then followed her sisters. She

didn't know what had gotten into Renata, but she was different, so much so that she hardly recognized her. Perhaps her older sister was going through early menopause as their mother had done. Moselle Wolcott claimed her menses had stopped before she'd celebrated her fortieth birthday. Tiffany decided to stay away from both her sisters. After all, she was the one with the perfect husband, home and children. But, she had to admit that Tamara hadn't done too badly with Duncan Gilmore. In fact, when it came to his looks she'd hit the proverbial jackpot.

They'd just entered the space with the panoramic views of the Hudson River when a loud, "Surprise!" rang out. Turning, Tamara caught a glimpse of her father's shocked expression as camera flashes went off, capturing the moment for posterity.

Daniel saw his three daughters standing together with their arms around one another. Shaking his salt-and-pepper head he blew out his cheeks.

"Speech, speech," a deep voice shouted.

"I need a drink," Daniel announced. "And make it a double."

"But, you don't drink, Daddy," Tiffany called out.

"But I do tonight," he countered. Everyone laughed. Daniel walked over to a portable bar, his guests following.

Tamara stayed behind with Duncan. "I've never known my father to drink hard liquor. Beer has always been his speed."

Wrapping an arm around Tamara's waist, he pulled her against his body. "There's always the first time for everything. It's not every day someone turns sixty."

"You're right, darling. It's quite a milestone birthday."

Duncan stared over Tamara's shoulder at Daniel Wolcott. The college professor was a commanding figure, standing several inches above six feet. He'd cut his thinning hair close to his scalp, while affecting a neatly barbered salt-and-pepper mustache and goatee. The gray hair shimmered against his mahogany-brown skin.

"Was your mother in on the surprise?"

"We had to tell her, because she's the only one who could get Daddy to come into the city. When he's not at school, all he wants to do is sit in his favorite chair and watch ESPN."

Duncan smiled. "He sounds like my kind of man."

"Here comes my mother."

He watched the approach of a tall, slender woman in sapphire-blue silk. The color flattered her skin, which reminded him of aged parchment. It was obvious the woman was mixed-race. Centuries ago she would've been presented by her mother at a traditional New Orleans octoroon ball.

Duncan wasn't one to prejudge, but the middle-aged woman gave off waves of snobbishness, and he prepared himself not to like her. Not

after what Tamara had told him about her judg-
mental nitpicking.

Moselle Wolcott patted her coiffure even though
not a hair was out of place. Her dark-brown eyes swept
over her youngest daughter. "You look nice tonight."

Tamara's stoic expression did not change when
she leaned forward to press her cheek to her
mother's. "Thank you. So do you—as usual."

Although shorter than Duncan, Moselle managed
to look down her long, thin nose at him. "Who do
we have here?"

"Mother, this is—"

"Duncan Gilmore," he said, offering his hand
while interrupting the introduction. "It's nice meeting you, Mrs. Wolcott.

Moselle took his hand. "You may call me Moselle."

He inclined his head. "Then Moselle it is."

Moselle released his hand. "Please excuse me, but
I would like to have a few words with my daughter."

Duncan walked away though it was the last thing
he wanted to do. He wanted to stay, stay and protect
the woman he loved. He moved a short distance
away and stopped. He couldn't overhear Moselle,
but he was close enough to watch the expression on
Tamara's face.

Chapter 13

Moselle pursed her lips. "Are you living with Duncan?"

Tamara almost laughed in her mother's face. "Are you aware of how old I am, Mother?"

An attractive flush suffused the older woman's face. "Of course I know how old you are. After all, I did give birth to you."

"If you know, then why are you getting into my business?"

Moselle refused to back down. "Because you *are* my business, Tamara. All of my children are my business."

"But there comes a time when a mother must respect her children as adults."

"I worry about you, Tamara."

"There's no need for you to worry about me. I can take care of myself. I've been taking care of myself."

"Wait until you have children, then you'll know how I feel."

"I don't know if I'll ever have children."

"But aren't you sleeping with that young man?"

Tamara rolled her eyes upward. "Mother, I know you didn't ask me that."

"Yes, I did, because I don't want you to make the same mistake with this man—"

"His name is Duncan, Mother."

Moselle waved a hand in dismissal. "Okay, Tamara. Duncan. I don't want a repeat of what you had with Edward Bennett."

"Now, when I look back on my marriage to Edward I can honestly say that I'm glad it ended the way it did, because it made me a stronger person. It taught me to be independent, to rely on no one but myself and, more importantly, it made me aware that I have to love myself before I can love anyone.

"I love Tamara Wolcott and I love Duncan Gilmore. He makes me laugh and he makes me feel good, Mother. I'm not living with him, but that's not to say that someday I won't live with him. He's the kindest and most generous man I've ever known. All

I ever wanted was for you to be happy for me, because I'm happy."

A beat passed as Moselle stared at the daughter she never knew. The daughter who refused to conform, the brilliant daughter who reminded Moselle of her own childhood when she'd had a weight problem, an ordeal she didn't want her own daughters to go through.

She held up both hands in a gesture of surrender. "All right, Tamara. I promise not to meddle in your business."

Tamara smiled. "Thank you, Mother."

"Your young man…"

"What about him?"

"What does he do? Where does he live?"

In a move that surprised herself, Tamara touched Moselle's cheek with her fingertips. "The next time you and Daddy come into the city I want you to have dinner with me and Duncan. Then you can ask him all the questions you want."

Moselle's pale eyebrows matched her graying light-brown hair. "But will he give me answers?"

"That I don't know, Mother. I suppose you'll have to wait and find out."

Moselle's left hand covered the one on her cheek. "I'm proud of you, Tamara. I don't know if I ever told you that."

"Yes, you did."

"When?"

"The day I became Dr. Tamara Wolcott."

Moselle flashed a wry smile. "Why is it you never were Dr. Bennett? You were still married to Edward at the time."

"Two Dr. Bennetts would've been very confusing, and as a medical professional I find the initials TB a bit disconcerting."

"Come, Tamara, let's join the others. And your young man looks annoyed because I'm monopolizing you."

Tamara watched her mother make her way to the bar. Her gaze swung to Duncan leaning against the wall, staring at her as if she were a stranger. He straightened with her approach, extending his arms as she came into his embrace.

"How did it go?" Duncan whispered in her ear.

"Okay."

"I've met your mother. Don't you think it's time I meet your father?"

Taking his hand, Tamara led Duncan across the room, feeling the curious stares directed at them. Nothing mattered because she was in love.

Using Duncan for support, Tamara leaned against him as she slipped out of her shoes. The birthday party had been a rousing success. An open bar, cocktail hour followed by a sit-down dinner with a live trio playing tunes from several decades…it had been an evening of frivolity that would linger in the memories of Daniel Wolcott and his guests for years.

Once the toasts were out of the way couples got up to dance while reminiscing about where they were or what they were doing when a particular tune was popular. She had danced with her father, her brothers-in-law and when she found herself in Duncan's arms she stayed. She, Tiffany and Renata settled the bill and it was almost eleven-thirty when Tamara and Duncan sat in the limo for the short drive to Chelsea.

"How are you feeling?" Duncan asked. He took off her jacket, dropping it on a chair in the living room.

She swayed slightly. "I think I had one too many flutes of champagne."

"I forgot you can't hold your wine," he teased.

She swatted at Duncan, but his reflexes were too quick and she missed him. "You're not supposed to mention that."

Duncan shrugged out of his jacket, leaving it on the chair with Tamara's. "I'm going to check on Duchess, then I'll be up."

Tamara tried putting one foot directly in front the other as if she were undergoing a sobriety test and failed. She didn't know why she had little or no tolerance for wine. "You're going to have to help me upstairs."

Duncan stared at Tamara's lopsided smile. He hadn't thought she was intoxicated, but it was apparent that she was unsteady. He approached and swung her up in his arms. "Poor baby can't hang."

She closed her eyes. "You've got that right."

Carrying Tamara with a minimum of effort, Duncan walked into his bedroom and placed her gently on the bed. "Don't move. I'll take care of you."

Tamara lay staring up at the shadows on the ceiling from the shaft of light coming from the streetlight. She wanted to get up and close the drapes but didn't trust her legs to support her.

She must have dozed off until she felt the warmth of a body next to hers. Duncan had undressed her. "I need to brush my teeth."

"I'll bring you your toothbrush and a cup of water."

He'd closed the drapes and she heard rather than saw him move off the bed. She brushed her teeth and rinsed her mouth with a solution of mouthwash in a half a cup of warm water. She swished the solution in her mouth, then spat it in the cup.

Duncan had promised to take care of her—and he had. He'd taken better care of her in a month than Edward had done in their six-year marriage. She scooted closer to him when he returned to the bed.

"How's Duchess?"

"She's good."

"Did she shred her wee-wee pad?" The puppy had begun tearing up the pads when left alone for long periods of time. The absorbent fibers stuck to her fur and getting them off was time-consuming.

"Not this time. Daddy told her he was coming back soon, so she decided to be a good girl."

"She's a good girl for you, but not for me."

"That's because you don't spoil her."

"Just how are you spoiling her, Duncan?"

"I give her a treat whenever she does her business on the wee-wee pad."

"But that's bribery."

"That's positive reinforcement, Tamara. Didn't you learn that in experimental psychology when you had to train the little white rat to run the maze to get a pellet of food?"

"There's such a thing as overdoing it, Duncan. If she gets too fat then you're going to have to get up early and take her for a walk every morning."

Turning over to face Tamara, Duncan rested his arm over her hip. "Why are we talking about a dog as if it were a child?"

"She's not a child, but she is my baby."

"And you're my baby," Duncan said in a soft voice.

"I'm your lover," Tamara corrected.

"Lovers who make love yet aren't in love."

"That's not true, Duncan."

"What are you saying, Tamara?"

"I love you."

Duncan snorted. "You love me, you love it when I bring you flowers, you love Duchess and you—"

"Stop it, Duncan. I do love you. I love you and I'm in love with you."

There came a beat, only the sound of the runaway pumping of her heart echoing in her ears. Tamara swallowed a groan. What was wrong with her? Telling a man she loved him when he hadn't given any indication her affection would be reciprocated.

"Where are you going?" Duncan questioned when Tamara sat up.

"Away from you." She was sitting up and a nano-second later Tamara found herself on her back with Duncan straddling her. "Let me up, Duncan."

"Not yet." Supporting his weight on his elbows, he pressed closer. "Not until I have my say."

"What?"

"Zip it, Tamara."

"It's zipped," she mumbled through compressed lips.

Shaking his head, Duncan couldn't help but laugh. "What am I going to do with you?"

"Huh-umm," she mumbled again.

Reaching between their bodies, he sandwiched a hand between her thighs. "I love your laugh, your smile and the sound of your voice," he whispered in Tamara's ear.

"I love your hair, the flawlessness of your skin.

"I love the way you smell and the feel of your skin against mine.

"I love your passion and your passion for life.

"I love your patience and your compassion.

"I say all of the above simply to say that I love you, Tamara Wolcott."

Tamara felt like crying. Looping her arms under his, she clung to him like a drowning swimmer grasping driftwood after a storm. "Show me, darling, how much you love me."

Duncan's hand moved up to her furred mound, fingers parting the moist folds. He felt her heat, inhaled the rising sexual scent peculiar to Tamara— an aphrodisiac that excited him, took him to incredible heights of passion and a natural sensual bouquet he was loath to wash from his flesh.

He took his leisure arousing her, tasting, touching, licking every inch of skin, beginning with her mouth and continuing downward to her feet. His tongue had become the brush of a master artist, outlining, tracing and painting a portrait that would endure throughout the ages.

He would endure in perpetuity along with Tamara through their children and their children's children. Never had Duncan felt the pull of fatherhood as he did at that moment. When he spilled his seed he didn't want it rejected by a synthetic hormone that inhibited conception, he wanted a new life, a rebirth of a spirit without the demons that hadn't permitted him rest or peace.

Tamara knew somehow that this coupling was different. She felt the tension in her lover's hands, the erratic beating of his heart, the uneven sound of his breathing. Closing her eyes, she ran her palms up and down his back, alternating the motion with kneading the muscles in his strong neck.

They reversed positions, she moving atop Duncan. She often assumed the dominant position, and whenever she did, Tamara reveled in the sense of power it afford her. Cupping his face between her hands, she slanted her mouth over Duncan's, trailing light kisses over his jaw, chin, the sides of his nose. Her tongue traced the silky outline of his eyebrow, her breathing quickening and becoming labored. As she aroused his passion hers followed suit.

Her hands charted a course over the crisp hair covering his broad chest, the muscles in his rock-hard abdomen, the corded muscles in his strong thighs. She'd come to know every inch, muscle and plane of Duncan Gilmore's body. But there was one part, the one organ which brought her extreme pleasure, she hadn't sampled.

Sliding down the length of the enormous bed, she buried her face between his thighs and cradled his rigid sex. Her fingers opened and closed around the long, heavy, pulsing erection, then she lowered her head and took as much of him into her mouth as she could without gagging. Her tongue flicked up one side of his penis, then the other, while her hand opened and closed around the increasingly rigid flesh.

Duncan caught the hair splayed over his belly, fingers tightening when Tamara suckled him so hard he feared exploding in her mouth. He swallowed a savage moan, then another, followed by another until he forcibly extricated himself from her mouth. She was breathing as heavily as he was when she settled herself over his groin, he arching and burying his erection inside her.

Tamara rode him like one possessed, setting a rhythm that took her and Duncan beyond themselves. Bracing her hands on his shoulders, she ground her hips against him in an attempt to get closer, to become one. Tamara being on top gave Duncan the advantage as he cupped her breasts, squeezing gently until she felt as though they would burst like overripe fruit.

She met his thrusts, her body moving faster and faster as rivulets of perspiration pooled between her breasts to trickle down to her belly and still lower. A single gasp dragged from parted lips preceded a soft moan when the contractions began. They increased in intensity, overlapping one another when she threw back her head and climaxed, the orgasms holding her prisoner until she was forced to give in to an ecstasy so shockingly pleasurable she feared losing her mind.

Duncan reversed positions again, buried his face between Tamara's scented neck and shoulder and growled out the last of his passion as he collapsed on her heaving chest. He loved her, loved her enough to ask her to share her life and future with him, but he decided to wait.

Waiting until his heart rate returned to a normal rhythm, he moved off Tamara, bringing her with him as he pulled her to his chest. They lay together, legs entwined and fell asleep.

Duncan felt as if he'd stepped back in time as he wended his way through the people in his living room, looking for Tamara.

Kali, more than he, had loved entertaining. If they didn't host a small get-together on an average of once per month, then she sulked, declaring she hadn't felt alive.

He'd told her he liked having friends over, just not so often. He didn't mind friends hanging out to watch a game or movie, but a constant flow of people who dropped by because they hadn't any other plans had begun to grate on his nerves. Duncan had humored Kalinda, hoping once they were married the parties would stop. They would open their home to family and friends on holidays or special occasions.

During his counseling sessions with Ivan, Duncan had come to understand himself *and* the relationship he'd had with Kalinda better: his need to please, her need for acknowledge. The parties represented a sense of freedom and purpose for the young woman to whom any expression of frivolity had been looked upon as wicked.

He found Tamara in the kitchen with the caterer.

Catching her eye, he motioned with his head; she nodded in acknowledgment. Seconds later she joined him in the pantry.

This afternoon they, like their guests, wore ubiquitous New York City black. The rain that had begun Friday afternoon had continued steadily throughout the night and into Saturday. However, the gloomy, wet weather did little to dispel the mood of the people who'd come together to celebrate the engagement of Kyle Chatham to Ava Warrick.

Tamara smiled at Duncan, finding him incredibly handsome in a white shirt and black slacks. The invitations had indicated casual attire and she'd selected a pair of black stretch cropped pants, a matching off-the-shoulder pullover and ballet-type shoes.

"What is it, Duncan?"

"Your friend Rodney is here."

He'd asked Tamara to invite her roommate to even out the male/female ratio. Ava had invited a social-work intern from her social services agency and Duncan hadn't wanted the young woman to feel out of place when most of the guests had come as couples. All of the employees in the Harlem brownstone were invited and most had confirmed their attendance.

Going on tiptoe, Tamara brushed a kiss over his mouth. "I love you," she whispered.

Wrapping an arm around her waist, Duncan pulled her flush against his body. "Love you back."

Pushing gently against his chest, Tamara winked at him. "We'll continue this later."

She walked out of the kitchen and into the living room where people were either sitting and talking quietly to one another or were standing around holding drinks or small plates of appetizers. Tessa Whitfield-Sanborn had ordered banquet tables and chairs set up in the expansive living room to accommodate the overflow of people not seated in the formal dining room with seating for ten. A bar was set up in the niche under the winding staircase, and the caterer had his waitstaff circulating, offering hot and cold hors d'oeuvres as soft jazz music came through the concealed speakers.

Simone Whitfield-Madison had come the day before with floral arrangements that were breathtaking. Ava loved pale pink and white flowers and the colors were repeated in the tablecloths and napkins and candles on tables and flat surfaces throughout the first floor of the duplex.

Tamara spied Rodney off to the side surveying the scene. Overhead light made his cropped hair appear more blond than red. He, like the others, wore black. The color enhanced his slimness.

Crossing the room, she reached for his hand. "I'm glad you could make it."

Rodney leaned down to kiss Tamara's cheek. "Thanks for inviting me. No wonder you hang out here. It's very nice."

"You can tell Duncan that after you get something to eat and drink." She glanced at her watch. "We're going to sit down to eat in another half hour."

"Something smells wonderful."

"That's the prime rib. You'll have a choice of beef, chicken or fish."

Rodney followed Tamara over to the portable bar and ordered a beer. "Duchess and I are really bonding."

Tamara narrowed her eyes at her roommate. Friday morning she had taken Duchess to her apartment to introduce the puppy to her new home. She'd known the dog would be traumatized by the noise and the incessant ringing of the doorbell on Saturday at Duncan's. When she opened the crate the ball of white fluff had run straight to Rodney. It was obvious the tiny bitch preferred males.

"Bonding how, Rodney?"

"She slept in the bed with me."

"No," Tamara groaned. "That's what I wanted to avoid."

"I couldn't get any sleep with her constant whining, so I did the next best thing and put her in bed with me."

"When are you moving out?"

"I hope before the end of next month."

Rodney had found a co-op in East Harlem highrise overlooking the East River with views of the bridges connecting Manhattan with Queens and

Brooklyn. He was waiting to close on his current apartment to finalize the sale of the Harlem property.

"There's someone here I want you to meet."

Rodney halted in the act of bringing his glass of beer to his mouth. "Who?"

"See the young woman with the black skirt and black-and-white striped top?" He nodded. "She's going to be your dining partner tonight."

"What's her name?"

"Maribel Vargas. She's a graduate student at Fordham's School of Social Work. She's interning at Ava's agency. I'll introduce you to her."

Kyle and Ava had arrived before their guests, giving Tamara and Duncan an overview on who was who and their relationship to the engaged couple.

Rodney took a sip of beer, staring intently at the social worker's legs, ending in a pair of stilettos. Without warning she turned, and he caught a glimpse of the face that went with the curvy compact body; he liked what he saw—a profusion of curly black hair, delicate features in an olive-brown face and a pair of large hazel eyes that sparkled like semiprecious jewels.

"You don't have to do the introductions. I think I can handle this on my own."

"Go, playa," Tamara said softly.

She watched as Rodney walked over to Maribel, leaned over to whisper something to her, and then extended his free hand. The look on the woman's face spoke volumes. She shook his hand, smiling demurely. Resting a hand in the small of her back, Rodney led her over to a chair, seated her and then sat beside her.

"What are you smiling about?" asked a familiar voice.

"Look at my roommate and Ava's intern."

Duncan stared at the man leaning in to hear what the pretty social worker was saying. "Maybe he'll propose marriage and move the hell out of your place."

"Stop it, Duncan! I told you there's nothing going on between me and Rodney."

"He looks a little too slick to be a doctor."

"How are doctors supposed to look?"

Duncan kissed the nape of her neck. Tamara had brushed her hair off her face and secured it in an elastic band. "The ones I know look like straight-up nerds and that goes for the men and the women."

"I've never been mistaken for a nerd," Tamara countered.

"There's nothing even remotely nerdy about you, Dr. Wolcott." He rested a hand on her hip. "Everything about you is sexy."

"You'd better stop feeling me up before someone sees us."

"And what are they going to say?" he whispered in her ear. "I'll turn off the music and the lights and herd them all the hell out of here."

"There's no need to go mad-hard," she chided, smiling.

Duncan moved closer, close enough for her to feel his stirring sex. "Keep talking and something will get *mad*-hard."

Tamara was saved from replying to his ribald comment when Tessa came over to tell her that her cousin was parked downstairs and wanted someone to come down and bring up dessert. Faith McMillan continued to bake cakes despite her advancing pregnancy, but had curtailed the number of cakes she usually baked for her demanding clients.

"I'll go down," Duncan volunteered.

"Take Micah with you," Tessa said to his back.

The noise in the duplex decreased appreciably when everyone sat down to eat. Ava and Kyle's immediate family and closest friends occupied the dining-room table while coworkers and the employees and their spouses and partners who worked in the Harlem brownstone housing the law, accounting and counseling firms sat at the round tables, becoming better acquainted with one another.

The chef had outdone himself with slices of succulent prime rib, fall-off-the-bone baked chicken and grilled salmon. The waiters were on hand to refill water and wineglasses. The five-course dinner was followed by an assortment of pastries that were the perfect complement for gourmet coffees and teas.

Duncan stood up and tapped his glass with the edge of his knife to get everyone's attention. All eyes were trained on him. "As best man for the groom of the couple we're honoring tonight, I'd like to thank everyone for coming out in this weather. I'm going to make this very short when I say…"

"Cut the bull—"

"Careful, Campbell," Kyle warned softly. "There are parents here."

Ivan extended his glass to Kyle's parents, then Ava's. "Sorry about that."

Frances Chatham narrowed her eyes at Ivan. "I can't believe you're still a cusser, Ivan Campbell, after all the times your mother washed out your mouth with soap."

Ivan dropped his head. "You're not supposed to mention that, Mrs. Chatham."

Everyone had a laugh at Ivan's expense, while his date leaned over and kissed his forehead, eliciting more laughter.

"As I was saying before the cusser interrupted me," Duncan continued, trying not to laugh, "Kyle and Ava, I know when I told you I wanted to host a little something to bring your friends and coworkers together you said you didn't want anyone to bring a gift. Of course we didn't listen. However, we managed to find out the names of your favorite charities, which incredibly happen to be the same." Reaching for an envelope beside his plate, he handed it to Kyle. "There's a bank check in that envelope made out to the United Negro College Fund. The donors are listed as Kyle and Ava Chatham. So you better get married, or the names on the check will constitute a fraud, counselor."

Kyle opened the envelope, his eyes widening in surprise. Rising to his feet, he leaned over and hugged Duncan. "Thanks, brother."

Duncan thumped his back. "You're welcome, brother."

Kyle showed Ava the check, then kissed her passionately. Ava passed the check around the table as the tempo of the prerecorded music picked up. The celebrating didn't end with dinner, but went on for several more hours.

It was close to midnight when all of the food was put away, the rented tables and chairs were gone and the dishwashers in the main kitchen and the second kitchen hummed as they went through the wash and rinse cycles.

Tamara took a shower and crawled into bed, falling asleep as soon as her head touched the pillow. The only thing she remembered was telling Rodney, as he was leaving with Maribel, to look in on Duchess.

The rain had stopped and the sun was high in the sky when she woke Sunday morning. It was the last day of her vacation and sharing dinner with Duncan's aunt would signal the end of her social season.

She never thought she'd admit it, but she looked forward to returning to the orderly chaos in the E.R.

Chapter 14

Tamara felt an instant affinity for Viola Gilmore when the older woman ignored her hand to kiss her cheek. And the love Duncan professed for his aunt was apparent whenever he looked at her.

Viola might not have given birth to Duncan, but the resemblance between them was remarkable, which indicated that Melanie Gilmore had been a beautiful woman.

Duncan, who'd rented a car for the day, convinced Viola not to cook because he was taking her to her favorite restaurant, the River Café, which overlooked the East River and the Brooklyn Bridge. Music and the sound of raised voices drifted up from the outdoor deck below the restaurant's dining room.

Tamara ate sparingly because she'd eaten so much the night before. When she'd put on her slacks she'd had to suck in her belly. So much for having a second helping of tiramisu and petit fours. She could maintain her weight *if* she skipped dessert. Like an addict, she couldn't just eat one, but tended to binge. Again, she reminded herself that going back to work was a good thing.

Duncan drove them back to his aunt's brownstone for coffee and dessert. Tamara accepted the coffee, but passed on the dessert. She sat in Viola's parlor, listening as the schoolteacher told stories, going back more than forty years, of her wonderful career as an educator. Duncan had excused himself to go over to Micah's house to discuss Kyle's February wedding. Kyle had selected Micah and Ivan as his groomsmen.

"More coffee, Tamara?"

"No, thank you, Ms. Gilmore."

Viola waved a hand. "Please call me Viola. Only if I don't like people do I insist they call me Ms. Gilmore."

"What if I call you Miss Viola?" She'd been raised never to address older people by their given name.

"I would prefer Aunt Viola."

Tamara smiled at the petite, elegantly dressed woman—she had paired a gray wool gabardine pantsuit with a white silk shell. "Then I will call you Aunt Viola."

Viola decided she liked Tamara Wolcott better than she had her nephew's late fiancée. Although Kalinda Douglas had died tragically, Viola didn't mourn the young woman's passing as much as she mourned for her nephew. His grief, which to her was akin to guilt, lingered far beyond a normal time for mourning the death of a loved one.

"You're the first woman Duncan has brought around since his fiancée died."

Tamara closed her eyes for several seconds in an attempt to process what she'd just heard. She hadn't known Duncan had been engaged to be married. "How…how did she die?"

Viola shook her head. "She was one of thousands who died on 9/11."

"Oh, please, no."

She felt her heart stop, then start up again with a beating that hurt her chest. The horror of that day was imprinted on her brain. She'd just walked into her pathology class when the first plane had hit. A voice over the PA system had said that classes were cancelled for the day, but Tamara didn't know what had happened until another student, who'd been listening to the radio, announced that the country was under attack.

Edward had switched gears from teacher to practitioner when the call went out for medical personnel to treat the dying and injured. Her husband had returned after a four-day absence a changed man. He rarely spoke and when he did he was monosyllabic. His bizarre behavior had continued until Tamara suggested he seek counseling.

Viola exhaled a breath. "Duncan took her death very hard. They were to be married that weekend. I think what exacerbated his grief was it took weeks to find her body—or what was left of her. What I found so strange was that he wouldn't cry at her memorial service. He sat motionless, staring into space, refusing to talk."

"Did he ever go for counseling?"

"He wouldn't for years even though Ivan Campbell made himself available to Duncan at any time or any day, but my nephew refused. He kept blaming himself as a boy for his mother's death, and something must have happened between him and Kalinda, because he hinted to me that he wanted to call off the wedding. But a week before 9/11 he changed his mind. Kalinda's parents were beside themselves because they'd paid thousands to hold the reception at the Hudson Terrace."

Covering her mouth with her hand, Tamara feigned coughing. It was no wonder Duncan was so subdued at her father's birthday celebration. No doubt he was reliving the time when he and his fiancée were given a tour of the venue as they planned what was to become one of the happiest days of their lives.

"Did he see other women after his fiancée died?" She wanted and needed to know if there had been other women in Duncan's life after Kalinda and before her.

"It was some time before he'd admit to me that he was going out with a woman. When I suggested he call a young teacher at my school because she'd expressed an interest in him, he said he would consider it if she was like his Kali. If not, then forget it."

For the second time within a matter of minutes Tamara felt a stabbing sensation around her heart. Unknowingly she'd become a replacement for a dead woman. The only thing worse would be if she and his Kali looked alike. Forcing a cold smile that didn't reach her eyes, she reached for her coffee cup and took a sip of lukewarm brew.

"Let me freshen up your coffee. It's been sitting there so long that it must be cold," Viola offered.

"No, please. It's okay. Duncan told me that this school year will be your last," she said, smoothly changing the topic of conversation.

Viola flashed a wide grin. "Yes, it is."

The two women were still talking when Duncan returned. He lingered long enough to drink a cup of coffee then kissed his aunt, promising to see her before the end of the month.

Duncan stopped for a red light and glanced over at his passenger. "Why so quiet, baby?"

"I don't feel like talking."

A slight frown appeared between his eyes. "Did my aunt say something to upset you?"

Shifting on her seat, Tamara glared at him. "Why didn't you tell me you were engaged, Duncan?"

The light changed and he took off. "It had nothing to do with you."

"Oh, really," she sneered sarcastically. "I spill my guts about the men in my life and you tell me a woman whom you loved enough to propose marriage to has nothing to do with me. Well, let me tell you this, Duncan Gilmore. I'm not into substitutes."

"What the hell are you talking about?"

Tamara clamped down her temper. "Stop the car, Duncan, and pull over." He kept driving. "I said stop this damn car and pull over—now!"

Glancing up at the rearview mirror, Duncan signaled and maneuvered over to the curb. Before he had a chance to react, Tamara had unsnapped her belt, opened the door and was standing on the curb hailing a taxi.

He pushed a button, lowering the passenger's-side window. "Get back in the car, Tamara."

Not bothering to look at him, Tamara walked down the street, her hand held aloft. A streak of yellow skidded to a stop, and she got in and gave the taxi driver her address. Reaching into her tote, she turned off her cell.

It had nothing to do with you.

If it had nothing to do with her then she would have nothing to do with Duncan Gilmore. The man who'd professed to love her, who wanted her to move in with him was reluctant to talk about his past. Duncan Gilmore was no different than Edward Bennett.

She hadn't known that Edward had had two ex-wives until she sat across the table in her lawyer's office.

And she hadn't known that Duncan had planned to marry another woman until his aunt told her. There was a good reason why she'd hadn't dated or slept with a man in four years. She couldn't trust them.

Tamara paid the cabbie and went upstairs to her apartment. She opened the door and was met by her whining, wiggling canine companion. "What are you doing out of your crate? Did Uncle Rodney let that girl out?"

Rodney strolled into the entryway. "I leave the crate unlatched, and she goes back in when she wants to use the wee-wee pad. I think it's time you snap the pads into the frame and put it where she can find it whenever she has to do her business. Every time I have to bend down to clean the crate I run the risk of throwing out my back."

"I'll start tomorrow because I'll be home during the day to monitor her." Duchess, now sleeping throughout the night went on her hind legs for Rodney to pick her up. "Sorry, girl, but Uncle Rodney has to leave for work. I'll see you tomorrow." Retrieving his knapsack from a hook in the entryway closet, he slung it over his shoulder. "I want to thank you, Wolcott."

"For what, Fox?"

He winked at her. "For introducing me to Maribel."

Tamara returned the wink. "I take it you like her."

"She's nice, very cute and very, very smart. And more importantly she's not into drama."

"Good for you."

Rodney nodded. "You and Duncan are an awesome couple. I wish you guys the best."

There is no best, she mused, closing the door behind his departing figure. Even Dr. Rodney Fox, whose love life mirrored a Spanish-language soap opera, had tired of the drama and moved on. Why, Tamara thought, couldn't she?

The distinctive ring of her telephone startled Tamara. Glancing at the display of the handset on the table, she recognized Duncan's number. Bending slightly, she picked up Duchess and made her way to her bedroom.

She fell across the bed, her puppy snuggling against her ribs, and went to sleep.

Duncan waited three days before he sought out Ivan Campbell. He was still in a quandary as to his relationship with Tamara. He'd called and left voice-mail messages on her cell and her home phone. She hadn't called him back. Knocking lightly on the open door, he waited for Ivan to look up and acknowledge him. A slow smile deepened the grooves in the psychoanalyst's lean face.

"Come in, DG."

Duncan walked into the opulently appointed office that reminded him of a living room. Leather sofa, chairs and chaise, table lamps and area rugs created a homey look. Whenever Ivan was in session, he always closed his door and turned off the overhead lights, leaving only the lamps lit to create a soft, calming effect.

Of the three friends, Ivan was the least formal. Most times he came to work wearing a short-sleeved shirt sans tie, slacks and occasionally a jacket. However, he did keep a supply of shirts, ties, suits and underwear in a closet for times when he had speaking engagements. He claimed "dressing down" made his patients feel comfortable enough to open up about their problems.

Ivan gave Duncan a look he usually reserved for his patients. "What's wrong, DG?"

"We need to talk."

Rising, Ivan walked over and closed the door. "Let's sit over there." He pointed to two facing chairs.

Duncan told Ivan everything—leaving nothing out about his relationship with Kalinda Douglas and Dr. Tamara Wolcott. "I can't lose her, Ivan. I refuse to give her up without a fight."

Ivan had known Duncan thirty-two years, yet the

man sitting in his office was one he didn't recognize. Although he'd made himself available to his friends, professionally he found it difficult to be objective. He knew too much about them.

He mentally shifted gears and within seconds he didn't see DG, friend, but Duncan Gilmore, patient.

Chapter 15

"Dr. Wolcott, they're bringing in a three-year-old male with broken arms and head trauma. Step-dad claims the boy was jumping on the top bunk and fell off the bed."

Tamara ripped off her latex gloves and slipped on a new pair. "Put the patient in room four and page Dr. Rodney Fox—stat!"

An intern rushed into the room carrying a small bundle, placing it gently on a stretcher. "Where's the mother?"

"He says she's at work."

She didn't think she would ever get used to treating the tiny patients who came in with broken bones from falling out of cribs or off the chair or down a flight of stairs when their parents were doing other things. The day before a frantic mother had brought in her toddler who'd fallen headfirst into a tub of hot water, sustaining third-degree burns over half the baby's body. As a doctor she was required to report the incident to the police, and as the child was airlifted to a burn unit at a Bronx hospital the frantic mother was read her rights and led away in handcuffs.

She'd tired of the excuses: *I only looked away for a second. I didn't shake my baby.* Or, name-blame of *He did it, she did it.*

Tamara worked quickly, checking the child's vitals. When she cut the tiny T-shirt off to avoid moving the little boy's arms, she froze. Bruises, old and fresh, dotted the chest.

"Oh, my heaven!" a nurse whispered on seeing the bruises.

"Get a cop in here," Tamara ordered through clenched teeth. There were police personnel on a floor where prisoners were brought in and detained for medical treatment. The nurse left and seconds later Rodney pushed his way through the interns standing around observing Dr. Wolcott.

"Who the hell did this?"

Tamara gave him a warning look. "The boy's step-father said he fell off the top bunk and hit his head."

Rodney had seen that particular look many times

before when he was called to examine a child. He turned to a nurse. "Call radiology for a CT scan."

Without warning the drape parted and a man reeking of alcohol crowded into the room. His dreadlocked hair was covered with lint and every inch of his muscled arms were covered with tattoos.

"What's with my boy?"

"I'm Dr. Fox and I'm taking your son up to radiology to take pictures of his head and body."

Bloodshot eyes wavered between Rodney and Tamara. "You don't need to take no pictures. Just patch him up and I'll take him home to his mama."

Tamara moved over to distract the obviously distraught man, giving Rodney enough time to take the child up to radiology. "Sir, we have to see if there's any head trauma before we can treat your son."

"Ain't talking to you, *bitch!* So stay the hell outta this."

Rodney stepped in front of Tamara to shield her from the man who literally had blood in his eyes. "Sir, please. Dr. Wolcott is right. Now, please step aside so I can give your son the medical treatment he needs."

The man shuffled to his right, but when he spied two uniformed police officers coming toward them, he lunged at Tamara, his arm tightening around her throat. Despite his state of intoxication he whipped out a knife and hit a button on a switchblade. The point of the blade bit into the soft flesh of Tamara's neck. A drop of blood appeared.

Tamara slumped against his muscled body, then righted herself as a rush of adrenaline shocked her system. Her heart kicked into a higher gear when she realized the officers had drawn their weapons.

"Drop the knife and let her go," the shorter of the two ordered.

"Get the baby out of here, Fox." Tamara issued her own order. She knew the man couldn't do anything to prevent Rodney from taking the child to be X-rayed as long as he held her hostage.

Duncan arrived at the entrance to the hospital to find it surrounded by police personnel. A female sergeant stopped him. "I'm sorry sir, but you can't go in now. We have a police situation."

He wanted to ask what the police situation was but he knew she wasn't going to divulge any information. Walking over to where a small crowd had gathered, he sidled up to a woman in a nurse's uniform who was talking to another woman wearing a lightweight jacket over a pink uniform.

Duncan's blood ran cold when he overheard them talking about a hostage situation taking place in the E.R. The nurse's cell rang, and she answered it.

"What's going on inside?" she asked. "No! He has a knife to Dr. Wolcott's throat threatening to kill her if the police don't put down their guns," she told her coworker. "The police have called in a hostage negotiator," she continued, relaying the information from someone inside the E.R.

Duncan had heard enough. Walking to the corner, he sat down on the concrete, unmindful of his tailored suit, and rested the back of his head against a traffic box, then he did what he hadn't done in years—he prayed.

He wasn't certain how long he sat on the sidewalk, but when he heard cheering he came to his feet. Rushing back to the entrance, he saw the same female officer. "Sergeant Whalen," he said, reading her name tag, "I know I can't go in, but could you get word to Dr. Tamara Wolcott that her fiancé is outside waiting for her."

"What's your name?"

"Duncan Gilmore."

The officer gave him a long, searching look. "Callahan, come over here." A fresh-faced officer who looked as if he'd just graduated the academy approached his superior officer. "I want you to get word to Dr. Wolcott that her fiancé, Duncan Gilmore, is waiting outside for her."

"No problem, Sarge."

It seemed like an eternity though in reality it was two hours later that Duncan saw Dr. Tamara Wolcott walk through the doors and out into the coolness of the early autumn night. It was the first time he'd seen her in scrubs and a lab coat. He saw her look around, then turn to go back into the hospital, and he moved quickly, sprinting across the street.

"Dr. Wolcott."

She turned and looked at him as if he were a stranger. "Duncan."

He took a step, bringing them closer, and that's when he saw it—there was a small white dressing on the right side of her neck. "Baby."

She smiled. "Duncan. You came. How did you know?" The news media had just arrived to gather the details of the hostage situation for late-night reporting.

"I came earlier to see you, but the police wouldn't let me in. I didn't know what was going on until I overhead a conversation between a nurse and someone inside the hospital."

Tamara's gaze softened. *I love you so much. I've missed you so very much.* "Why did you want to see me?"

"I want to tell you about Kali."

"You don't have to, Duncan. It doesn't matter anymore."

"Yes, it does matter, baby. It matters because I love you. I love your very life and if anything had happened to you I don't know what I would've done. Every woman I've ever loved I've lost. It started with my mother and then with Kali. I want it to end with you, Tamara."

"And how is that going to happen?"

He closed his eyes. "I want to marry you."

Tamara felt weak in the knees, fearing she was going to collapse, but she recovered quickly. She'd spent two hours with the blade of a knife to her neck and now Duncan had followed one shock with another by proposing marriage.

"We'll have to talk about it, Duncan."

A smile curved Duncan's mouth. He was still in the running—Tamara hadn't openly rejected his proposal. "When do you want to talk?"

"Tonight. I was clocking out when the police officer told me you were here. Let me go and change and I'll be out."

Tamara and Duncan lay in bed in the East Village apartment, talking quietly as so not to disturb the little dog sandwiched between them. Duchess was beyond spoiled. When she saw Duncan she whined incessantly until he picked her up.

Tamara listened without interrupting as Duncan told her about the sad young woman he'd rescued from an oppressive childhood.

Even though Kalinda Douglas had lied to him Duncan was willing to forgive her because she so feared losing him. What Tamara had communicated to him was that though she'd feared losing him, she knew she would eventually recover enough to turn the page.

Duncan traced the gauze bandage on her neck. "Did he cut you?"

"No. He broke the skin when he pressed the point of the blade too hard. There was just a trickle of blood. It's true when people say that before you're going to die your life flashes in front of you."

"Did it?"

"No." There was a hint of laughter in her voice. "I thought about you. I tried imagining being married to you. Then, when I fantasized about screaming for drugs once I went into labor with our baby I started laughing hysterically. I must have shocked the man holding the knife because when he dropped his arm the police rushed him. They must have gotten in a few punches while trying to subdue him because he needed medical treatment."

"Do you really want to be drugged during labor?"

"Hell, yeah, Duncan. Why play super-heroine?"

"What if I'm there with you? I promise I'll keep you calm."

"I'll have to think about it."

"Think about what, Tamara?"

"Whether I'd want you in the labor room with me."

"That can only become a possibility if you marry me."

Shifting onto her side, Tamara stared into the warm depths of the eyes gazing back at her. "You're right about that. I remember that you, Kyle and Ivan took an oath that you didn't want to be baby daddies."

"You're right. I wouldn't know my father if I passed him on the street, but I can assure you that my children will know their father."

"How did we go from a child to children?"

"Remember, I'm an only child."

Running a finger down the length of his nose, Tamara's mouth replaced her finger when she kissed him. "No, you're not. You have Ivan and Duncan."

"You're right. They are my brothers."

"Ask me again, darling."

Duncan stared at Tamara under lowered lids. "Ask you what?" he teased.

"Ask me to marry you."

He took a deep breath, then let it out. "Tamara Wolcott, will you do me the honor of becoming my wife?"

Her eyes met his, seeing love and her future in the large gold-brown orbs. "Yes, Duncan Gilmore, I will marry you."

He leaned over to kiss her, but disturbed Duchess who got up, shook herself then jumped straight for Duncan's chest. She turned around and around before settling down to go back to sleep.

"What the…heck!" Tamara sputtered. "I never thought I'd have to share my man and my bed with another female."

Throwing back his head, Duncan laughed loudly. "Maybe she needs her own man."

"Are you talking about getting another dog?"

"Why not, baby? After all, we have plenty of room."

Tamara thought of the number of rooms in the Chelsea duplex. "True."

Then came a beat. "When does your lease expire?" Duncan asked.

"June. Why?"

"How would you like to become a June bride?"

"That sounds good."

"Where do you want have the wedding?"

"I've always dreamed of having a wedding aboard a ship. Do you think we can get the *Celestial?*" Tamara wanted to relive her first date and first kiss with Duncan.

"I'll call tomorrow to see if we can reserve one of the private rooms. If they're booked up then I'll rent a yacht for the wedding and honeymoon. We can use the ship as our hotel when we sail to different Caribbean islands."

Tamara kissed him again. "I like the sound of that."

"I thought you would," he said against her moist, parted lips. "I told that police officer that you were my fiancée. I think it's time I stopped lying and made it a reality. Let me know when you can get a day off to go shopping for a ring."

"I'm off tomorrow." She touched the bandage on her neck. "Workers' comp."

"How long do you think you can stay out and milk the system?"

Tamara shrugged a shoulder. "That all depends

on my therapist. After all, I did experience emotional trauma and anguish."

"Who's your therapist?"

"Dr. Ivan Campbell. But he doesn't know it yet."

Duncan laughed at the top of his lungs, and Duchess raised her head to look at him. "Damn, she rolled her eyes at me."

"That's what you get when you have two women in your bed. You have to deal with the fallout."

Tamara closed her eyes and said a silent prayer of thanks. She'd never known when she'd found herself trapped in a highrise elevator that the man trapped with her would become a part of her life and her future.

She was more than fortunate.

She was blessed.

ROCHELLE ALERS

Rochelle Alers has been hailed by readers and booksellers alike as one of today's most popular African-American authors of women's fiction. With nearly two million copies of her novels in print, Ms. Alers is a regular on the Waldenbooks, Borders and *Essence* bestseller lists, and has been a recipient of numerous awards, including a Golden Pen Award, an Emma Award, a Vivian Stephens Award for Excellence in Romance Writing, a *Romantic Times BOOKreviews* Career Achievement Award and a Zora Neale Hurston Literary Award. A native New Yorker, Ms. Alers currently lives on Long Island. Visit her Web site, www.rochellealers.com.